Guarded Desires
Uniform Encounters
Book 4

Morticia Knight

Knight Ever After Publishing LLC

Guarded Desires (Uniform Encounters 4)

Copyright ©2014, 2022 Morticia Knight

Second Edition

Edited by Barham Editorial

Cover design by Get Covers Design

Published by Knight Ever After Publishing LLC

All rights reserved. This literary work may not be reproduced or transmitted in any form or by any means, including electronic or photographic reproduction, in whole or in part, without express written permission. This book cannot be copied in any format, sold, or otherwise transferred from your computer to another through upload to a file sharing peer-to-peer program, for free or for a fee. Such action is illegal and in violation of Copyright Law.

All characters and events in this book are fictitious. Any resemblance to actual persons living or dead is strictly coincidental. Models are for representational purposes only and not related to the content herein.

All trademarks are the property of their respective owners.

All Rights Reserved

This literary work may not be reproduced or transmitted in any form or by any means, including electronic or photographic reproduction, in whole or in part, without express written permission. This book cannot be copied in any format, sold, or otherwise transferred from your computer to another through upload to a file sharing peer-to-peer program, for free or for a fee. Such action is illegal and in violation of Copyright Law.

All characters and events in this book are fictitious. Any resemblance to actual persons living or dead is strictly coincidental. Models are for representational purposes only and not related to the content herein.

All trademarks are the property of their respective owners.

Possible Triggers

On page violence plus graphic descriptions of murder. Kidnapping and peril. Domestic abuse.

Author's Note

Guarded Desires was originally published in 2013 under the same title with a different publisher. This edition has been re-edited and revised, but the story remains the same. Stephen and Joseph's story may also have references to places or events specific to the time period when it was written that are no longer relevant today.

Visit me at www.morticiaknight.com

A young National Guardsman, a snarky DEA Agent and a vicious drug cartel. Someone's going to be sorry.

Special Agent Stephen Morris thought his home life had settled into a pleasantly dull routine. Being assigned to a main border crossing in Arizona keeps him busy enough at work, so he doesn't have time to worry about love. However, that doesn't mean he's not lonely.

PFC Guardsman, Joseph Pirelli, is on an active-duty-for-training mission to help support border patrol and the DEA. The Vasquez drug cartel has become more ruthless than ever by targeting civilians on both sides of the border. Love isn't on Joseph's radar at all, either—especially not after being horribly abused by an ex.

Joseph and Stephen are thrown together in a direct conflict with the cartel and bullets fly with a startling outcome. Through it all, Joseph is drawn to Stephen, yet can't let go of his terrifying past. The idea of becoming close to a man who could physically harm him brings up fears that may ruin his chances at a relationship with the big teddy bear agent.

When shocking truths are revealed, both men fear they might lose the other. Can they escape the gruesome fate the cartel has in store for them?

Chapter One

"Are you fucking kidding me? Cheap piece of crap."

DEA Agent Stephen Morris wiped away the sweat dripping into his eyes and re-checked the current burner phone in use for the undercover deal. Agent Gonzalez hadn't contacted him yet and it was well past the arranged time. The phone's battery life was waning and here he was—stuck lying behind a clump of low scrub brush, trying not to scrape his arms over and over on the gritty dry ground.

Clean shirts with no tears are overrated.

The plan was for Rigo to contact him as soon as the deal was done, and alert him that he was on his way back to pick him up. Once Rigo had the trust of the dealers, they would be able to do a large sting and take them down. But in the meantime, Stephen was holed up in a remote desert locale near the border in Arizona, wondering where the hell his partner was.

Initially, there hadn't been any indicators that this low-level marijuana operation was connected to the Vasquez Cartel in any way—the cartel that had been like an insidious presence ever since it had positioned itself as the newest force to be reckoned with. The Mexico-based alliance had everyone on edge.

In hindsight, he wished he'd been more insistent that Rigo not go in alone. It was dicey when they did this type of undercover gig, but it had been deemed a waste of resources to use one of their deep undercover guys. Rigo did local stuff only and everyone at their home base teased him about being a master of disguise. Stephen was a great balance, more of the investigative backbone of their partnership.

Having worked as a Drug Enforcement Special Agent for close to ten years, he was accustomed to anything and everything happening. There was no such thing as the norm. But what should have been a fairly routine operation now seemed more and more like a really bad idea.

Stephen detected something in the distance and grabbed his binoculars. *Dust clouds.* They were increasing in size and heading his way, the approaching vehicle traveling at a fast clip.

He whipped out his Glock 23 pistol in case it wasn't his partner and double-checked it for readiness. He moved to a crouching position, maintaining his cover, ready to either fire or make a hasty exit. More sweat blurred his vision and stung his eyes, and Stephen cursed the pre-summer heat as he swiped at his forehead again.

The vehicle was almost upon him, and Stephen could tell it was the undercover car—a black late model Chevy sedan complete with a couple of small dings and dents to reinforce Rigo's persona as a minor player dealing weed and the occasional prescription narcotics in one of Tucson's suburbs. He wasn't ready to breathe a sigh of relief quite yet. The car barreling ever closer was newly decorated with numerous bullet holes and a cracked windshield.

The Chevy ground to a stop, sending larger clouds of dirt

Guarded Desires

and gravel into the air. The passenger side window rolled down a tad.

"Let's go. Now!"

Stephen launched himself from his position, staying low and yanking open the door before leaping into the car. Even as Stephen slammed the door closed, Rigo gunned the engine. No explanations were needed. That could wait for later.

Stephen had his weapon ready. "Should I be covering us from the back?"

"Yeah. Do it."

Stephen turned in his seat to watch for pursuers, closing the window to keep the dust from choking them. It was next to impossible for him to see anything with the dirt clouds billowing behind the bouncing, jostling, racing Chevy. Stephen held onto the back rest to keep from being tossed about so much.

If this thing survives its desert abuse, it'll probably be rewarded with a trip to the junk heap.

At last, they made it to the access point from the highway and Rigo fishtailed onto the road, regained control and floored the sedan. Now that they were off the dusty terrain, Stephen could get a view of where they'd come from.

He couldn't see any vehicles approaching from the desert, but before he holstered the Glock, he rolled the window down again and checked for any helicopters advancing on them. Even though the operation had originally seemed to be a basic, low value sting—in light of Rigo freaking out and the bullet hole detailing on the car—he wasn't taking any chances.

"Are we clear? Are we clear?" Rigo's eyes were wide as he stared at the road ahead and gripped the wheel.

Stephen turned around in his seat and buckled his belt, still holding the Glock at the ready. "We're good, buddy. Now, what the fuck?"

Morticia Knight

* * *

One more beer then I'm getting the hell outta here.

As soon as Rigo returned from the pisser, Stephen planned to tell him he was done for the day. What had gone down earlier had been way too close as far as he was concerned. The last thing Stephen wanted was to lose a partner on an assignment. In the close to ten years he'd been with the DEA, that had never happened—and he wasn't about to let it happen now.

"Hey dumbass, don't look so happy."

Stephen frowned, in no mood for their usual bullshitting. "Love you too."

"Sorry. I only like the kitty." He held up a hand as if to stop Stephen from commenting further. "I know, I know—don't know what I'm missing, right?"

After sitting in one of the rickety chairs, Rigo took a long swig of his Tecate beer, dragged his sleeve across his mouth, then set the nearly empty bottle down.

Typically, Stephen would have had an equally smart-ass comeback, but something unnamable churned in his gut. He wasn't superstitious, and he didn't have any particular religious leanings, but he did believe in intuition to a certain degree. He'd been on the job long enough and had completed enough field assignments that he knew when something was off.

"Okay. One more time. They didn't even give you a chance to start the deal? They just had you in their sights right away?"

"I'm tellin' you man, they knew. They fucking *knew.*"

"And there's absolutely nothing you can think of that could've tipped them off? Even the tiniest comment or gesture —anything?"

"Nice vote of confidence there, *partner.*"

"It's okay, you can cry. Let it all out. I won't tell the guys back at the station."

Guarded Desires

"I only cry when I think about your love life. That's a true tragedy. But to answer your question, it went how it always does. They were practically begging me to do business with them before today."

Rigo was one of the best agents he'd ever worked with, but people still made mistakes. However, he also knew that if Rigo had tripped up somehow, the man was not above admitting to it.

"I don't get it. All our intel on these guys was very low-key. They aren't connected to anything or anyone hardcore."

"Yeah, but obviously they are now. Either they're trying to increase their street cred or they've just been recruited by our new guys."

Stephen shook his head. "Fuck. Vasquez's reach seems unstoppable. The way things have been going lately, I've got to assume this is their work. We need to check and see if there've been any new messages sent from them in the last couple of days while we've been nose deep in our operation."

A message from the cartel never entailed anything written. It typically involved severed heads or bodies where evidence of the worst types of torture were apparent.

"I'm gonna get another beer."

He didn't check Rigo's reaction, he simply pushed up from the table, forcing the abused wood bar chair back as he did. It dragged loudly on the equally beat-up wood floor.

Rigo grunted. "Yeah, thanks. I wasn't going to get another one anyway. What is your problem, homey?"

Stephen ignored him and strolled up to the bartender of the El Gringo Loco lounge. The bar was a mixture of shabby Southwest décor from sometime in the sixties and newer Mexican tourist trinkets. It was an absolute dive with two pool tables, a dart board, long bar, a couple of cracked pleather booths and wobbly Formica tables. The dry desert heat was probably the only reason the old beer that had soaked into the carpet for years hadn't turned into black mold, yet the stale hops smell remained as a memento that the dried liquid was indeed still there.

As Stephen leaned against the counter waiting to be served, he absent-mindedly glanced around the room. A tall and slender young man approached the bar, catching Stephen's eye. He moved with a confident gait, but his eyes were cast down as if he were purposely avoiding engaging anyone in conversation. As he reached Stephen—two barstools over—Stephen was able to get a better look at the man.

Why am I looking anyway?

The last thing he wanted to do was be obvious. It was hardly the time or place to be picking anyone up, but something about this man appealed to him. He didn't usually go for younger guys, but there was a maturity in how he presented himself—as if he wouldn't take crap from anyone—and that always turned Stephen on. Plus, this man was hot. Exactly the type Stephen was attracted to. The tall, fit frame was alluring to be sure. But Stephen could also see a strong chin and sharply outlined masculine features as he took in the young man's slightly angled profile. His look was completed with shortly cropped dark hair.

I wonder what color his eyes are.

No doubt the kid was straight, and likely one of the local border agents or guardsmen who had just been sent in. He'd heard that the new active-duty-for-training group had arrived earlier. They would be switching out with the last group leaving and work with the Border Agents for three weeks until they were changed out again.

Ever since the Vasquez Cartel had gotten so completely out of control, as many reinforcements as possible had been called

Guarded Desires

in. The ordered had come from the highest level of government as the terror grew in the border towns.

At first, it appeared to only be an escalation in assaults on the Border Agents. That was always a danger for them, and would fluctuate between quiet times with little activity, then spurts of violence. But in the past few months, four men had lost their lives in gruesome, seemingly pre-meditated attacks. It was at that point that his own investigation into this newer cartel had led him and his partner Rigo to believe that the border agent attacks were part of a much larger picture.

Then the violence had gone beyond agents.

American and Mexican citizens of all backgrounds were being attacked and killed in the border towns. Signs pinned to the corpses warning the authorities to 'back-off' reinforced their intent. None of the victims could be tied to drug smuggling or any other gang or illegal activities. Many had been innocent women and, disturbingly, children.

What was even more frightening was that the murders were increasing and more often than not, happening on US soil. The Guardsmen had been brought in to help protect the citizens and stem the panic, while the DEA and Border Patrol continued their job of hunting down the animals who were responsible for the killings. Cooperation between the American and Mexican law enforcement agencies had never been stronger.

At last, the bartender wandered over to take his order.

"Another Tecate?"

Stephen nodded. He'd been holding his wallet as he'd waited for the drunk at the end of the bar to quit talking the server's ear off. He opened it and slapped a five-dollar bill down on the scratched up counter. After closing his billfold, he stuffed it into his back pocket.

The server turned to the young man. "I'll need to see some ID."

Stephen glanced over at the kid who seemed none too pleased. He pulled out a military card and held it defiantly in front of him for the bartender to see.

The server nodded. "What'll you have?"

"Bud Ice."

"I only have bottles."

"That's fine."

He threw down some cash, and Stephen noted that he left the bartender a buck as a tip. A lot of the younger guys weren't very good at giving decent tips—if they gave any at all. It impressed him somehow.

"You coming or going?"

The kid regarded him with a puzzled expression as if wondering whether the question was actually directed toward him.

"Excuse me?"

I think those eyes are a darker blue.

"I noticed your military ID. Are you in the group arriving, or are you on your way out?"

"Oh. Yeah. Uh, just getting here."

He seemed a bit uncomfortable, not making eye contact and Stephen wondered why. True, Stephen knew he appeared intimidating—about six foot two and bulked up—but he wasn't right next to him.

"Well, we can use all the help we can get right now."

"You Border Patrol?"

"No. DEA. Name's Stephen by the way, Special Agent Stephen Morris." He moved closer and extended his hand. He could swear he saw the kid swallow a little before taking it with a nice firm shake.

That would feel good fisted around me.

Guarded Desires

As the thought came to him, his cock twitched.

"Joseph. Joseph Pirelli. Nice to meet you."

This is a scintillating conversation.

For some reason he wanted to keep talking to Joseph and maybe find out if he was straight or not. His gaydar had never been that great, and he hated meeting guys under vague circumstances.

"Hey, dumbass! That was Boyd. He wants a rundown of earlier. I'm headed to the car, so suck that beer down and let's go."

Stephen held up a middle finger as an acknowledgment without even glancing Rigo's way.

Dammit. Oh well, probably for the best.

"As you can see, the honeymoon's over. Partners." Stephen rolled his eyes dramatically and Joseph chuckled. "It was nice to meet you, too. Maybe I'll see you around."

Stephen took a long, hard swallow of his beer, not moving his gaze from Joseph then set the bottle down. He noticed that Joseph had also stared at him the entire time and it had him wondering. Of course, his parting statement had sounded rather flirty. It could be a good sign.

"Yeah. Maybe you will."

Stephen arched his eyebrows.

Guess I'm not the only one who sounds flirty.

He nodded to the kid and meandered out the door, imagining Joseph staring at his ass the entire time.

I need to make sure and pay this dump a visit again. It suddenly has a lot more appeal.

* * *

Fuck yeah.

The bear of a man who had just introduced himself had

Joseph's mouth watering. As Stephen left, he couldn't stop staring at his tight, muscular butt. It had been nicely wrapped in a pair of dark jeans, along with his powerfully built thighs. He didn't even want to get started on Stephen's biceps. He already had to hide his boner by scooting all the way up to the bar.

The agent's eyes were a nice hazel color, he had light brown, close-cut hair, and he sported a neatly trimmed goatee. He was a bit older than what Joseph typically went for, but otherwise, he was the hottest piece of man meat he'd seen in a while. And he was sure the big man was gay.

Is he interested?

It certainly seemed as if was, but their meeting and conversation had gone by in a flash. There was just enough time to catch a little spark before he'd been called away by his partner. He figured that Stephen was only buddies with the partner and nothing more, but regardless, he was jealous that the guy got to spend time with the hunky Stephen.

Joseph gave himself a mental shake. What difference did it make whether Stephen was gay or interested? This was a three-week active-duty assignment, then he would be on his way back to Mesa, Arizona. He had some vacation time coming after which he would either find out what his next orders would be or volunteer for yet another active-duty assignment.

Maybe come back to the border?

He couldn't do that to himself. He'd been so careful to stay out of trouble after what happened with Dorian. And relationships were nothing *but* trouble. Stephen might seem wonderful —strong and protective—but he was also big enough that if Joseph ever pissed him off, he could do real damage to him. The way Dorian had done.

Suddenly, the whole idea of fantasizing about the hot bear lost its appeal. The two years of being punched and kicked

Guarded Desires

around by Dorian were enough for one lifetime. He needed to get with a guy who wasn't so brawny. It seemed like a dumb way to consider a potential partner—'I could take you in a fight'—but he couldn't help it. The complete and utter vulnerability he'd experienced with Dorian was something he refused to ever repeat.

He was in a different place now. He'd risen above his circumstances in so many ways. The experience with his ex-lover—the only relationship he'd ever had—combined with being bullied and teased in school had taught him two important things. He needed to stand up for himself and to not come off as vulnerable.

To that end, he'd worked out to get his naturally lean body stronger and defined. Learning kickboxing had helped even more. Finally, entering the military had not only given him some direction, but had built his confidence. He also hoped it added to the impression that he was not to be messed with.

Recently, he'd become ashamed by his initial motivation for signing up to be a guardsman. Some of the worst heavy flooding during the monsoon season in Arizona's history had hit a while back, occurring in a rural area with several small towns. Many people had either lost their lives, their homes, or gone missing. The men from his platoon had been sent to help sandbag, dig through debris to search for survivors and to deliver medical supplies and food.

The experience had greatly changed his outlook. He'd begun to take pride in what he did, grateful for the opportunity to make a difference.

Joseph took another swig of his beer and glanced around the sketchy bar. The place was pretty empty and his original intent of getting away from his fellow guardsmen seemed unappealing now that the brawny agent had vacated the dive. Not socializing much with his fellow enlistees helped avoid too many personal inquiries into his life. He didn't want to talk about babes, brag about bar fights, diss various groups of people or a lot of the other stuff that the guys from his unit did.

So far, his love of basketball had been the only decent conversation he'd shared with anyone. But even that had been sullied. There were two guys in particular from his group who stuck together. Their predominant not-so-clever banter involved using every gay slur known to mankind. Any basketball player who fucked up a play was either gay, a pussy, or whatever other slam they could conjure up. Even if the rest of his unit didn't openly go along with them, they didn't do anything in the way of opposing them either. It would just make his life simpler and more stress free if he kept to himself.

Joseph finished his beer and figured he might as well walk back to the house where he'd been assigned for his stay. The guard kept a few places rented out near the Nogales Armory for the extra revolving troops, at least until the current local need was exhausted.

Joseph carried his own fantasy that maybe the bloodshed would end while he was on duty. Being a part of stopping the ruthless cartel plaguing the local area would be worth anything the two assholes he was assigned with could dish out. Too bad he couldn't throw in a little R&R with a certain hunky bear as well.

Chapter Two

Stephen gritted his teeth, taking a calming breath before responding to his boss.

"Look, Boyd, I hardly think we were out of line."

Boyd dragged a hand across the top of his head. "Morris, I think you guys are top notch. You're my best. But we can't keep fucking up like this. The higher ups are gonna have my ass here pretty soon. I listened to what Rigo had to say and I still think you guys missed something out there."

"Fine. Then what would you suggest?"

Special Agent in Charge Boyd leaned back in his desk chair, his hands folded behind his head. This was his trademark 'deep in thought' pose. Stephen prepared himself for the interminable wait that he would likely have to endure, as the man insisted on complete quiet when formulating one of his self-proclaimed brilliant ideas.

When Stephen transferred to the Tucson sector from Massachusetts, he'd initially been impressed with Boyd. His boss had treated him with respect and encouragement. But now that he'd lived and worked in the border town of Nogales for almost two years, he saw another side to the man.

Boyd wasn't a yeller, and never came across as outwardly loud and obnoxious. He had a quieter, craftier way of pushing his agenda. There was a way about Boyd where he he'd been able to lull him and Rigo into thinking they were holding more power than they actually did. Yet he was continually behind the scenes, striving to orchestrate every move, and if it served his purposes, to allow credit for a job well-done to be passed on to whomever he needed to get in his court.

The prior year had been a perfect example. He and Rigo had taken out a key player in a Tucson meth ring. The operation had involved several months of investigatory gymnastics to make happen. A newer agent working on their team who was a family member of one of the Boyd's superiors, had ended up receiving an award at a splashy ceremony for his part in the whole operation. Stephen and Rigo had barely been acknowledged—not even a 'good job' from their direct supervisor, or anyone else involved with the case.

Neither Stephen nor Rigo wanted an award. That aspect had nothing to do with why they did what they did. They didn't even necessarily need a whole bunch of pats on the back. However, having someone who'd been an ancillary member of their team receive all the credit had been a slap in the face.

The acknowledgement would've also been nice for their career advancement if that tribute had been put on their records. For that reason alone, Stephen had approached Boyd to discuss the situation. The lieutenant had talked around and around the issue, a master at diversionary conversation, until finally he had gotten it through to Stephen to back off or else.

In so many words anyway.

Stephen sighed loudly and Boyd eyed him with a frown.

"I think your best course of action is to head down to the

Guarded Desires

section on the east side of town near the main towers. That's close to at least three of the main subterranean tunnels. If I were you, I'd have pairs stationed around the entire area. Not only does it get regular activity, but you'll have some support from the group of guardsmen that just came in. There'll be two in a Humvee with some gear. I think you and Gonzalez could make some headway there."

Stephen pursed his lips. *Stupid.* "Is that such a good idea?"

Boyd lowered his arms and leaned in, resting his arms on his desk. "You don't think the patrol knows their job?"

Boyd phrased his question in such a calm and soothing way. He came across as though Stephen were nothing but a confused and misinformed child.

"I'm not questioning the patrol, sir. I understand that there's a lot of activity there, but recently it's been primarily lesser groups. For our investigation into the Vasquez Cartel, Gonzalez and I have identified some possible unmonitored areas where new tunnel construction may be occurring—"

"Yes, Morris, I read the report from you and Agent Gonzalez. I think your theories have merit. But in case they don't pan out, I'm going to assign Agent Spender with several other Guardsmen to that spot and place you and Gonzalez in charge of the main locale. I wouldn't want my best agents to waste their time. Anything else?"

Boyd graced Stephen with what he figured was the lieutenant's practiced ingratiating smile. Once Boyd had mentioned Spender, Stephen knew that he and Rigo were toast as far as their theories were concerned. Obviously, the award hadn't been enough.

Stephen knew their investigative work into possible border access points the cartel might be using was solid. Solid enough to give the new agent another chance at accolades off their hard work.

When this is fucking over, transferring out. I'm obviously spinning my wheels here.

"No, sir. There's nothing else."

* * *

"Come on, Pirelli. It's not that late. There's a titty bar not too far from here. We can get in one good night out on the town before we start this assignment."

Joseph was in the process of unpacking his gear while his bunkmate continued to pester him.

"You're too young to drink."

Alex grinned. "But not to look at boobs."

Joseph pursed his lips. "You said it was a bar."

"This place caters to military guys. You have to get a wristband to drink, but you only have to be eighteen to stare at—"

"Boobs. Yeah, I get it. Look, Alex, I already went out to get a beer, so I'm good. I just wanna relax tonight before we head out tomorrow evening. I'm not in the mood."

"But that's just it. We only go on morning briefing, then we have the afternoon free to sleep it off before we head out on our first assignment. This is our last chance before we're officially on duty. The whole unit is going. It's perfect."

"Not when I have to get my ass up at the butt crack of dawn, it isn't."

"Jesus, Pirelli. If you don't start hanging out with the guys once in a while, you'll have Barnett and Griffin ragging on you, claiming you're a fairy and shit."

Joseph snorted. "I don't give a fuck about those two Neanderthals."

"Can't say I disagree, but you know how easy it is to get on the wrong side of people. As long as we're all stuck here with each other, it'd be good to socialize."

Guarded Desires

Joseph muttered under his breath, "I doubt that—"

Loud banging on their door was accompanied by grunts and hollering.

Speaking of Neanderthals...

"Hey, Pirelli and Yuen—are we gonna go see some big titties or what? Let's go!"

"Yeah, bitches—if I don't see some huge knockers soon, it won't be pretty!"

Griffin and Barnett took off down the hallway to yell and bang on more doors.

Alex gestured to the closed door. "You see what I mean?"

Joseph rubbed his face. "Listen. My stomach is kinda upset. I probably drank my beer a little too fast or something and I haven't eaten much all day. I just wanna lie down, okay?"

Alex shook his head in what seemed to be bewilderment. "If you stay here, you're going to be left with nothing but MREs. No other food's been brought in yet."

"Is there any of the meatloaf?"

He actually liked some of the meals ready to eat.

Alex gave him a horrified look. "I certainly hope not. That shit is vile."

Joseph laughed. "More for me then. You go on ahead."

Alex shook his head. "All right, man, but be prepared for some ribbing later."

Joseph shrugged. "That's cool, I don't care. You have a good time and tell me all about it."

Or not, if I'm really lucky.

* * *

Stephen mulled over everything that had happened over the course of his very long day. The TV droned, he had a cold beer in his hand, and his feet were propped up on the couch. One of his favorite X-Files reruns was playing, but he wasn't paying much attention to it. The background noise helped him think.

One of the main things he was considering was how glad he was that he hadn't bought a house. Instead, he rented a small two-bedroom, one bath home when he first arrived. The little bungalow had a nice yard he could barbeque in and was tucked away at the end of a quiet street.

As much as he'd hoped that Nogales would be a semi-permanent stop, it no longer appeared that way. He liked Arizona quite a bit, even if it was so different from where he was from. There was a less hurried feel to it that appealed to him. And of course, he had a great friend in Rigo.

But with the ongoing drug problems for all the border states, it wouldn't be too much trouble to find another assignment in the state. Especially with his strong track record and high marks from Quantico—in spite of the recent slight he and Gonzalez had experienced.

He certainly didn't have any relationship concerns to consider. The guy he'd been vaguely serious with right before he moved hadn't been willing to discuss any type of relocation. They'd remained friends on Facebook, but when Stephen invited him to come and visit, his ex had made excuse after excuse. He finally admitted he was seeing someone else and that was that.

Stephen finished his beer then set it on the coffee table next to him. He tried to avoid thinking too much about romantic possibilities. He was plenty busy with work and he and Rigo had a solid friendship. His partner invited him over quite a bit to hang out with his wife and two kids. Stephen was famous for his barbeques and had Rigo's family over as well, along with other co-workers. His social life was decent.

But he was fucking lonely. And horny. Even if he hadn't been head over heels for Henry, they'd had a comfortable rela-

Guarded Desires

tionship that included regular sex. It hadn't been mind-blowing and passionate sex, but hell, he'd certainly take it over his right-hand man any day.

Plus, there wasn't any warmth at night—no one to sleep next to, kiss goodbye, or cuddle with on the couch while watching a movie.

Sighing, Stephen switched off the TV. Maybe he'd read a good crime novel in bed until he passed out. Perhaps another beer would help. He sat up, then scratched his head. Leaning with his elbows on his knees, the urge to get another beer brought his thoughts back to El Gringo Loco—and the young Guardsman, Joseph. The kid would never be more than a good lay, especially being so young. He was probably into hooking up with all kinds of guys. Stephen remembered all too well what he'd been like at that age. But would that be so bad? He'd seemed like he might be interested.

Stephen still wasn't a hundred percent sure Joseph was gay, but it couldn't hurt to go check that place out again. After all, they'd both said maybe they'd see each other around. *Yeah.* Maybe he'd stop on by the next chance he got.

* * *

The raucous arrival of his fellow Guardsmen woke Joseph from a dead sleep.

Damn, they are out of control.

If they were housed at the armory, he was sure there would be some pretty heavy recriminations. As it was, he couldn't imagine their CO not hearing about the shenanigans. And should there be consequences, it would be difficult to either prove or explain why he was the only one who hadn't gone along for the fun.

The door to his room burst open and his bunkmate Alex

stumbled in. He slammed the door behind him while singing Justin Timberlake's *Sexy Back* quite badly, then collapsed on his bed.

"You fucked up, homey! I'll admit I was just going along for the ride, but there were some damn fine bitches there tonight. You really missed out."

Joseph groaned. "Jesus Christ, Alex. Why do you have to talk like that? You sound like one of the gorilla twins."

"Ah, they're not so bad when you hang out with them. I know they're pretty crude and shit, but they know how to have a good time."

"Crude doesn't bother me. Being fucking disrespectful toward women does."

"So what are you now? Marching for women's rights?"

Joseph rolled over to face the wall. Alex hadn't thrown the light switch on when he'd burst in, but Joseph wanted to distance himself as much as he could from the only guy he'd hoped he could at least have a decent relationship with.

"I'm going back to sleep. If you have any brain cells left, you might want to do the same. We're due to get up in less than three hours."

Alex muttered something under his breath, then called out. "Okay, Saint Pirelli. I'll do as you command. Try not to be such a buzzkill next time."

Joseph quietly sighed. *I wish I was back in Mesa.*

He enjoyed the suburb and could stay with his mom out in Phoenix on the weekends or between non-active-duty training sessions. There was also a guy who'd been his original Battle Buddy during Basic, knew he was gay and was cool. They had hung out quite a lot. But then his friend had received orders for a twelve-month deployment.

Now, Joseph was on his own mission after there was a Presidential order for Guardsmen help at the border. Joseph had originally been excited about going—it would have been another way to help—but now he wasn't so sure.

Joseph tried to calm his mind so he could drift back to sleep. The light snores of Alex irritated the hell out of him. Not because they were loud in any way, but because his roommate had been able to drop off to sleep so easily after jolting Joseph wide awake—leaving him with his troubled thoughts.

Sometimes he got lonely with no one special in his life—at least his fantasy of what sharing his life with someone might be like. His only real relationship had been with Dorian, who had continuously beaten the crap out of him. Dorian had sweet talked him at first, but once Joseph moved in, everything changed. He seemed to get off on proving to Joseph over and over again who was really in charge.

In many ways, Joseph wasn't sure he truly thought of his time with Dorian as a relationship. In addition to the emotional and physical abuse, there had never been any affection between them. Dorian never even liked to kiss, let alone hug or hold him in his arms after sex.

Joseph could never label their physical interaction as making love, either. There was no love. Only Dorian's obsessive control over him and Joseph lying to himself in the beginning about what they were to each other. And eventually staying because he believed at the time he had no other choice.

Being eighteen and stupid really sucks.

If it was only when he was eighteen that he stayed, that would've been bad enough. However, Dorian had made sure to keep his hooks in Joseph for longer than that. Joseph even managed to get away from him for almost a month, but Dorian had tracked him down at his aunt's ranch near Flagstaff. Dorian had threatened Joseph that he'd hurt her if he didn't go back with him.

He'd known for a while that Dorian was mixed up in some

illegal shit, but had also known better than to ask questions. Typically, Joseph was kept in the back area of the house where he was expected to be ready to either service Dorian, be beaten by him, or both.

One of the best days of his life was when the DEA had burst through the front door of Dorian's place on the outskirts of Mesa and hauled his sorry ass off to jail. Joseph was arrested also, but it hadn't taken the DA's office too long to figure out that Joseph was a victim and not an accomplice. The fresh bruises and old scars on his body had been verification of that. That was what had saved him from a felony charge. Otherwise, his ability to join the military would've been taken away forever.

The DEA had played an integral part in his salvation that day, but he never had he seen such an incredibly hot agent as the one he'd met at the dive bar.

Just because he's a big guy doesn't mean he'd smack you around. Plus, he's one of the good guys. He's not a vicious pig the way Dorian was.

But how could he know that for sure? He'd exchanged all of three or four sentences with the guy. He wasn't sure if he believed in vibes or intuition or whatever you wanted to call it —but there was some sort of good feeling in those few moments with Agent Stephen Morris.

Joseph sighed out loud, knowing that Alex was dead to the world. It didn't bode well that he couldn't get the older man out of his mind.

I'm an idiot.

* * *

Stephen rubbed his forehead. "So, the only FLIR you have right now are on the towers?"

Guarded Desires

"*Sí*. The rest of the infrared equipment has been placed with the varying Agents out in the field tonight."

Stephen resisted frowning at the Border Patrol Agent who ran the Nogales division of the US Customs and Border Protection, or CBP. He knew their budgets were stretched paper thin and night vision equipment was pricey. They all worked on the same team, yet Stephen had more than a hunch that any expensive equipment from their office had been allocated to Agent Spender's mission—the one that he and Rigo should've been on.

Hey now. Don't get bitter, it won't help anything.

Lately, his little inner pep talks had been needed more than ever.

"Okay, Sanchez. I understand. What about our boys from the Guard? They usually have all the fancy gear."

"We're only getting two guys tonight. The rest are headed down to some secret locale with Agent Spender."

Stephen grunted. *Not that secret to me.*

"I would think at least one of them would be equipped with some Forward Looking Infrared? Or Night Vision goggles. A penlight perhaps? Two rocks and a stick?"

"I'm not holding my breath, *amigo*."

Stephen tried to stave off the blanket of negativity threatening to envelop him when Rigo approached with two large cups of coffee.

"Please tell me you put whiskey in those."

"Hilarious. I was hoping to get fired tonight too."

"What the fuck difference will it make?" Stephen took a deep breath to help dial back his irritation. "Sorry. I'm not trying to be an ass."

"It just comes naturally, right?"

Stephen drew his eyebrows together as he accepted one of the coffees from his partner. He couldn't blame Rigo. It sucked working a dead lead while pulling an all-nighter, and it was made even worse when he had a corner on the bad attitude market.

"Okay. I deserve that. Let's start over. Thank you for the wonderful coffee. Lovely evening we're having, isn't it?"

"Why yes, it is. Care to dance?"

Patrol Agent Hank Sanchez shook his head. "You might want to hold off on picking your dancing partners just yet. Here come our Guardsmen now."

Stephen turned around and almost dropped his coffee. It was the kid from the bar.

Joseph checked his gear, adjusting his patrol uniform and verifying everything was as it should be. He'd also packed the Humvee and was ready to go right on schedule. Joseph wasn't sure he could say the same for Alex. His bunkmate still seemed to be suffering from the previous night's jaunt. Even though Alex claimed that the place they went to wouldn't serve alcohol to minors, Joseph seriously doubted that. The possibility made him antsy about being assigned with Alex, if that were the case.

Regardless, Joseph wondered if Alex thought going out late had been such a wonderful idea after all. If the situation had been reversed and Joseph went to see some hunky male strippers, he wasn't sure he would've believed the sacrifice was worth it.

Then again, if that bear of an agent had been stripping down...

Joseph wanted to slap himself. He needed to remain focused on his first mission at the border, and the last thing that would encourage concentration would be imagining Agent Stephen Morris sans clothing.

Guarded Desires

"Yuen! We're going to get written up!"

They were at the Nogales Armory, and Alex had run inside to use the restroom before they left. He was meandering back to the packed vehicle but dragging his heels.

"I'm coming. God, you're pushy."

Joseph wasn't in the mood. At twenty-two, he sometimes felt like a senior citizen compared to a lot of the new recruits. It wasn't that there weren't those who were older than him, there had been plenty back in Mesa. But in his current group, it seemed the majority were either eighteen or nineteen years old. Which explained a lot about the previous night's little excursion into town.

At last, they climbed in. After checking out, they drove to their assignment. Once they pulled into the command center, they headed over to a group near one of the patrol towers. It was pretty dark right where they were, but it appeared as though there were three border agents huddled together talking. One of them was likely their lead. But after they exited the Humvee and drew closer, Joseph noted that two of the men were wearing Kevlar vests with 'DEA' emblazoned across them. The larger one glanced up and locked eyes with his.

Joseph sucked in a sharp breath. *I am so fucked.*

Even though it wasn't all that surprising they might cross paths out in the field or on an assignment, it seemed crazy that it had happened so soon. And obviously, Agent Morris recognized him since he was in the process of staring Joseph up and down. All of a sudden it was as if Joseph were exposed. He didn't want anyone else around—not when it was the first time they were seeing each other since their initial meeting.

Joseph licked his lips. He wanted Stephen. He didn't want Stephen. Which one was it? Maybe it wasn't that he didn't— but *couldn't*—want. He couldn't take the risk.

Alex nudged Joseph with his elbow. "Hey, look," he whispered, "it's Conan and his merry men."

Joseph huffed. "What does that even mean? Shut up and quit goofing around."

"Fuck you, Mr. Perfect. Try and chill out for once."

Agent Morris stepped forward as they approached. The brief hint of recognition Joseph had seen was gone from the man's face. But it was for the best. The evening's operation was hardly the time or place to acknowledge one another.

"Gentlemen, glad to have you on board. I'm Agent Morris, and this is Agent Gonzalez." Stephen indicated to his partner. "Border Patrol Agent Sanchez will be in charge of tonight's operation. And you two are...?"

Joseph stood tall, his back straight. "Private First Class Pirelli and Private Yuen."

Agent Morris raised his eyebrows. "PFC, huh?" A slight curl appeared at one side of Stephen's mouth. "All right, gentlemen, before Sanchez takes you through what you'll be doing this evening, I'm dying to know one thing."

Stephen's eyes were locked on him, and Joseph had a wild thought that Agent Morris was going to say something completely personal and unrelated to their mission.

"Sir?"

"Please tell me you have some FLIR in that clunky pile of metal you drove over here."

Joseph laughed out loud, and Alex furrowed his brow. "Yes, sir. I bet I have a lot that you could use."

Agent Morris cocked his head to the side and this time he curled his lips up into a full smile. Joseph realized too late that he might've spoken out of turn with too much of a double entendre. Heat moved its way up his face, and he was more grateful than ever that it was so dark where they were.

"That so? Then let's take a peek, shall we?"

Guarded Desires

"S-sure. Over here."

Joseph refused to lose his practiced stance—the one that said he wasn't intimidated by anything or anybody. Yet Agent Morris had almost managed to fluster him into doing just that. *More reasons to stay far away.* There had also been a subtle questioning gaze from Stephen's partner as he'd observed them both.

After their equipment had been checked out, Agent Sanchez went over the almost identical protocol and procedures they'd heard that morning from their CO. However, judging how out of it Alex had been during the earlier briefing, it was probably a good idea that everything was being reiterated.

The instructions were essentially a reminder that the Guard was there to back up the efforts of the Border and DEA Agents. They weren't authorized to apprehend or detain any illegal immigrants. The primary objective for that evening would be to partner with the DEA agents in counter-narcotics measures.

After that speech, they were given locations and what to be on the lookout for. It was typically very boring work where hours seemed to stretch into infinity. But he knew he could never let his guard down for even a second—just in case.

Joseph was assigned to patrol the east side of one of the main towers and Alex the west. They would only take the Humvee out farther into the desert terrain as the night wore on or if there was suspicious activity. Otherwise, it was strictly foot patrol. Joseph wasn't sure what the other agents were doing, and it wasn't his place to know. His only concern was to follow orders.

The FLIR relied on heat signatures by detecting the difference between the ground temperature and a person or animal. The towers were equipped with them, but they were of a limited range—only about five hundred feet. By patrolling with his night goggles, Joseph could detect movement outside that perimeter, as well as get a somewhat clearer indication of what might be moving around without relying strictly on heat temperature ratings.

As he scanned the horizon, he spotted Agent Morris not too far away by an outcropping of rocks. He couldn't let himself be distracted. There was no room for anything in his head other than his duty as a Guardsman. Anything else could come later —if at all.

The rest of his group was sent farther out in the desert on some special operation. They had left a half hour before him and Alex, and Joseph pondered that it might have been better if he'd been given that mission. Hopefully, if he had to return to this section again, Agent Morris would be far, far away doing something else—and not teasing Joseph with possibilities that should never be.

* * *

What a long-ass night.

Stephen checked his watch and noted that it was barely past two a.m. He still had another four hours to go, and it had been like a tomb out in the desert. He hadn't even heard a coyote cry and they were usually making a ruckus at this time of night.

His thoughts were drawn back to the start of the evening. Seeing the kid saunter up to him in full uniform with a confident stride had just about done him in. He'd never been the type given to random bursts of public arousal—at least not since high school—but seeing Joseph like that had almost caused an embarrassing moment.

Something struck Stephen about Joseph's manner, his

Guarded Desires

outward display of strength. He wore his uniform proudly. Stephen admired how someone that young could be so sure, so self-assured without coming across as overbearing. He had ambition—it was obvious from his ranking. But there had been that one moment when he'd stuttered.

He's worked hard to overcome something. He doesn't want anyone to know he might be vulnerable.

There was something inside Joseph that Stephen wanted to uncover. Whatever softness there was in Joseph had been damaged and Stephen imagined he could reach it. Coax it out of the young man without him feeling as if he was giving anything up.

Stephen pressed his lips together, wondering where the sudden urge to uncover Joseph's story came from. He shook his head. Who was he kidding? He knew damn well where it came from.

The need to protect went back to when he was a kid and his dad would use him, his mom, and his brother as his own personal punching bags. Stephen had inherited his father's physical makeup, but fortunately, not his temperament. By the time he'd hit fifteen and had bulked up in wrestling, his dad had thought twice about going after him.

The day Stephen laid his dad out for breaking his mom's arm was the last they ever saw of him. It was a source of anger and hurt that his dad's best friend had also been the town sheriff, so his dad had gotten away with way too much over the years. Once he'd become afraid of his own son, though, the little coward had taken off and never come back.

Fuck him. I wonder if this kid has been through something similar.

Stephen took a piss behind some bushes and wondered how long the Lieutenant would have him and Rigo out in the desert chasing shadows. So far, the only thing that had gone

29

down was a couple of small groups of illegals who'd been detained by some of Sanchez's men. They were being processed down at the small detainee building near one of the towers.

Stephen zipped his fly and gazed up at the abundance of stars. The night was clear and cool, even as they approached summer. A slight ripple of a breeze blew past him, and he thought he might like to go up to the Grand Canyon or somewhere before it got too overwhelmingly hot. He'd been there once when he first arrived. When people spoke of pictures not doing something justice, Stephen believed the canyon was the first place he'd ever seen where that phrase truly applied.

A shot echoed in the distance somewhere behind him. He dropped down by the rocks he'd strolled back to earlier and readied his Glock. Speaking into the radio attached at his shoulder, he tried to summon Rigo.

"I have activity behind me and to the east."

"I heard... Do we have any guys out there?"

Shit. Joseph.

"I think we have a Guardsman. Is Sanchez near you? I don't know where his men are."

"On it. You still in the same spot?"

Stephen kept his voice low. "Yes, but I'm moving in."

"Hold on. I'll bring the jeep over."

"There may not be time. One of our guys could be in trouble."

"Jesus, Stephen, you won't be able to see fuck all out there."

"I've got clear skies and good moonlight. I know this area. I'll keep you informed."

Stephen shut off his radio in order not to bring any attention to him in case someone was nearby. He followed the small desert path that had been well-worn by years of immigrants crossing the unforgiving terrain.

Guarded Desires

So many people lost their lives every year—some from the harsh conditions if they made the trek on their own, and some from the coyote smugglers who demanded a high price to get them across the border. If there were too many people packed into a vehicle and it crashed in a high-speed chase or was abandoned, they could die from their injuries or the elements.

More gunfire rang out, much closer this time. Stephen surged forward as his adrenaline kicked in. He found another group of small boulders and crouched down to get a better feel of his surroundings before he advanced any further.

"Eat shit, DEA scum."

Stephen gasped at the cock of a gun next to his ear.

This is it then.

A shot rang out.

Chapter Three

Joseph sucked in large gulps of air, barely able to control his breathing, his body shaking uncontrollably. His M16 rifle trembled in his sweaty hand, and he gripped it with all his strength, terrified that he would drop it on Antonio's dead body or accidentally discharge it.

Dead.

He'd never shot anyone before.

"Get this fucking piece of shit off of me!"

Agent Morris' voice brought Joseph back to the present and he rolled Antonio onto his back and off Stephen.

Jesus. He could've been killed. What the hell is Antonio doing out of prison?

The shaking increased. It had all happened so fast, so unexpectedly. Trying to keep focused, Joseph took his rifle off semi-auto and back to burst mode in case there were other threats nearby.

"Some help here? I think I fucked up my knee when I went down."

Joseph nodded, still breathing heavily and unable to bring

32

Guarded Desires

forth any words. He reached down and Stephen used his big paw of a hand to grasp Joseph's as he pushed himself up from the ground. Joseph was about six feet, but the agent had a couple of inches on him. Standing this close to him was heady —touching him even more so.

Joseph tried to release his hand, but Stephen didn't let him go. As Joseph had always known, the man was strong. His grip felt good, comforting. Joseph peered up at him.

"Wha...?"

Stephen clasped him tighter. "Thank you. I thought I was dead."

The agent squeezed his hand and pumped it a couple of times as if he had only ever meant to shake it all along.

"Was that him shooting at you or someone else?" Stephen continued.

Joseph cleared his throat. "Uh...not exactly either."

This was going to be difficult to explain. It could also potentially end his military career altogether. Still, he would do it again in a heartbeat if it saved Stephen's life.

Stephen pinched his eyebrows together. He didn't appear angry, only confused.

"I'm going to radio this in with our location. But do you want a minute to explain anything to me first?"

Joseph cringed. Of all the fucked-up things to be the subject of his first real conversation with Stephen. And with a dead body at their feet.

"It's... I... This guy..." Joseph groaned. "I know him."

Stephen's jaw dropped. "You *know* him? As in good buddies, your long-lost cousin, the guy who trims your hair —*how* do you know him?"

Joseph swallowed, trying to stand straight like he always did, maintain his assuredness. It wasn't working all that well.

"I need to sit down."

"Holy Jesus, kid. What is going on here?"

Joseph's knees wobbled and he knew the adrenaline was waning, that the reality of his predicament was sinking in. He extended his arm to his side and sank against one of the boulders. As he faltered a little, Stephen reached out and grabbed him, helping to ease Joseph onto the large rock.

Joseph peered up, sure that he'd see anger or disappointment from Stephen's eyes. All he could discern in the moonlight was concern.

"Sorry. I never shot anyone before." Joseph gave a forlorn little laugh. "I didn't think I'd be such a big baby about it."

Stephen placed a gentle hand on Joseph's shoulder, softly stroking it with his thumb. "You're not a baby. You're having a normal human reaction. That's nothing to be ashamed of."

Joseph nodded, giving him a weak smile.

The agent removed his hand and Joseph wished he hadn't. He wanted Stephen to take him in his arms, despite how ridiculous the idea was. Not only in that moment, but probably ever.

"I have to call this in, Joseph," Stephen said softly. "Is there anything else you want to say before I do?"

Joseph sighed. "Yes. That man was an evil fuck, and the business partner of my ex-boyfriend. But I'm in all kinds of trouble now. That wasn't him shooting at me." He raised his head, holding Stephen's gaze. "It was the other way around."

* * *

The paperwork alone on what happened in the desert was going to take half the day and the other half would be explaining everything to Boyd. Joseph had told Stephen briefly about who that Antonio character was, and a little bit of their history before Sanchez and Rigo arrived to pick them up.

Stephen also realized that Joseph was right. The kid was in

Guarded Desires

a lot of trouble. But he was going to do everything he could to stand up for the man who'd prevented Stephen's head from getting blown off.

It turned out that the dead guy had been involved with drugs and gunrunning a few years ago when Joseph was with someone named Dorian. After Dorian's operation was taken down, Joseph had been able to get away from what Stephen surmised was an abusive situation. Stephen hadn't pried, but his explanation confirmed Joseph was gay. That would now also be known to everyone else as soon as the complete debriefing was finished.

Being gay in the military wasn't an easy ride. Stephen had a close friend from high school who'd been through a very difficult time after enlisting in the army but had stuck it out. He'd eventually proven himself during the Iraq War by dragging several of his comrades to safety after their convoy had been attacked with RPGs and massive gunfire. Those who'd mocked him previously either had the guts to apologize or the sense to shut up from that moment on.

Stephen sensed Joseph's experience from that time in his life was part of what made him so intent on proving he wasn't weak. However, the immediate issue was getting the Guardsman out of trouble.

Sanchez stepped out of the office and approached Stephen. "I've contacted his commanding officer and he's on his way down. I'm not sure what's going to happen to him."

Stephen frowned. "He saved my life, Hank. I would literally be dead meat right now if he hadn't done what he did. That's gotta count for something."

"Yeah, I agree. It's just the way he went about it. Chasing a suspect all around the desert while shooting at him isn't exactly military protocol. Especially since the guy never shot at him first."

"Can I have a minute with him?"

"Help yourself. It'll take his CO a while to get here."

"Thanks."

Stephen entered the small, dingy room. A dreary yellow glow lit up the stark surroundings that were comprised of a long table, four folding chairs and a short counter with a coffee maker, microwave and a tray of cup o' noodle soups. Joseph didn't even look up when Stephen walked in. He maintained his posture where he sat but was partially turned away.

"Mind if I have a seat?"

Joseph shook his head, continuing to stare at the wall.

"Look. I'll never be able to thank you enough for what you did, and I'll do anything and everything I can to help you out, no matter what." Stephen folded his hands on the table and leaned forward. "But could you tell me exactly what happened out there? It seems like you've given the military ammunition to use against you by admitting that you shot at him before you even saw if he was armed. I don't understand why. Especially since I already know there's more to the story than you chasing what you thought could be an unarmed guy around with a gun. He was much more than that to you. What's this really all about?"

Stephen was shocked at how forthright Joseph had been. Many others in his position would have colored it in their favor. It had been two men out in the dark desert alone and one of them—a known criminal—was dead. It spoke of the young man's integrity that he hadn't pretended to be the hero in the situation.

Joseph shrugged, finally turning toward Stephen. "I don't want you to think badly of me."

Stephen shook his head in bewilderment. "My head is still intact and my brains aren't splattered all over the desert. I don't know how I could possibly think badly of you, no matter what you say." Stephen paused, weighing his next words. "I understand if you don't want to say anything more, I'm practically a stranger to you. But I really want to hear the complete story of what happened. I want to get to know you."

Joseph raised his eyebrows on Stephen's last remark. Maybe he'd gone too far by saying that, but he needed to draw Joseph out before his superior arrived.

"All right."

Joseph had spoken very softly, and Stephen's heart broke a little. It was the most vulnerable Stephen had seen the kid and he had the urge to take him in his arms and tell him everything would be okay.

Joseph sucked in a deep breath before continuing. "I thought I heard something and put my night vision goggles on. But it was strange. Judging from the sound, it seemed very close. Yet, as I scanned all around me, I couldn't see anything. That was when I realized it was coming from the ground, and I remembered all the info we'd gone over about the tunnels. I took the goggles off and crouched near where I suspected the opening might be. The second I saw Antonio emerge from the tunnel, I pulled my weapon on him."

Joseph's breathing sped up. "I saw him do some horrible things when I was with Dorian. In some ways, he was the worst between the two of them. Not in what he did to me personally. But I saw him rape and beat women, torture people who crossed him. He did try to go after me once, but Dorian threatened him. It was the only time the asshole ever stood up for me. However, it became clear it was because he wanted to be the only one who hurt me. It didn't matter whether it was fucking or punching—I was *his* property."

Stephen tried to keep his rage contained as Joseph revealed in a dispassionate voice some of the horror he'd had to endure.

He would've done anything within his power to protect Joseph from that prick.

Stephen fought to keep his tone even. "What happened after you pulled your weapon?"

"He laughed at me. Said I was nothing but Dorian's bitch and he wasn't scared of me. That I wouldn't pull the trigger but that he was going to go waste some agents and then come after me. Put me down like a dog, just as he'd told Dorian to do dozens of times before."

"You told all of this to Sanchez?"

"No way. Just the part where I saw him and shot without thinking."

"Dammit, kid. That's not the full truth. I figured you told them about Dorian—that this guy was in business with your ex-lover who's in the slammer."

Joseph grunted. "What? No fucking way. I can't bring all that shit up. Everyone will know I'm..." His shoulders slumped. "Shit."

"That you're gay? You'd rather be dishonorably discharged or go to prison than reveal you're *gay*? Do you think things will be better for you in the slammer?"

Joseph visibly paled. "Prison..."

"Exactly. What else happened after that? How did Antonio get to me?"

"I'm not entirely sure, but it was almost like he knew exactly where you were. He caught me off guard by darting away. I hadn't honestly thought he would blatantly ignore me while I held a rifle in his face. I fired off a round, but he'd bolted. I panicked because of what he'd said about wasting agents, so I chased him down. It seemed as though he had a specific agenda.

Joseph took a deep breath, his breathing amping up. "I fired again, but it was so dark where he was that I couldn't really see,

Guarded Desires

and I missed. I shouldn't have taken the goggles off. But I was able to catch up to him just as he was about, about to..." Joseph choked on his words.

Stephen was drawn to Joseph more than he'd been drawn to any man in a while. Joseph seemed to have a very full heart that had been closed off for a long time. He was strong, a fighter. Joseph had disregarded his own fears and any possible consequences for his actions. His only concern had been to keep Antonio from hurting any agents. There was no way he would go down for this.

"Own up to everything and we'll get you out of this mess. I'm not saying you might not still get disciplinary action, but it won't go that far." Stephen paused, making sure that Joseph held his gaze. "All I can think of right now is how incredibly brave you are. And how thankful I am that you were the one out there tonight."

"Really?" Joseph sounded so vulnerable.

"Yeah. Really."

A thought nagged at the back of Stephen's mind.

What did Joseph say? 'It was almost like he knew where you were.'

"Fuck!"

Joseph startled. "What? What's wrong?"

"Come with me, kid. I think we might have a problem."

Stephen dashed out of the door, Joseph on his heels.

"Rigo! Where's Sanchez?"

His partner regarded him with a scowl. "What's up? And why isn't he in the room waiting for his CO?"

"We don't have time for that. I need Sanchez to contact his agents at the other site—the ones with Spender."

"What? Why?"

"I think I know why the agents are getting picked off so easily."

And Boyd has just sent a buffet of men out into the desert to potentially be slaughtered.

* * *

Agent Morris, his partner, Gonzalez, and Alex rode with Joseph in the Humvee. Sanchez couldn't raise any of his guys at the other location, so they were racing there as quickly as they could. Even one of Stephen's fellow agents hadn't responded to the frantic calls.

Before they left, Sanchez had insisted that Joseph stay behind with Joseph's CO already on his way down, but Stephen had insisted that he needed both Guardsmen.

Joseph had to wonder why Stephen was so worked up. But judging from how on edge and insistent he'd been that they needed the Humvee, he figured they were headed into a firefight.

So far in his short military career, Joseph hadn't been engaged in any combat situations—unless they were simulated ones during training exercises. He was also still reeling from the grim scenario earlier. A part of him felt guilty that he wasn't sorry Antonio was dead, yet another part was grateful he'd been there to save Stephen. His gut clenched at the thought of losing him—even if he didn't really have him to begin with.

Joseph cast the errant thought aside, intent on what they might be running into at the other location. He was in Guardsman mode and not even the consequences of his earlier actions mattered at the moment.

"Here." Stephen pointed ahead. "Coming up—you'll see an access point on the right. Rigo marked it with a flag."

Joseph noted the small wood stake with a strip of red fabric tied to it as his headlights flashed across it. He steered off the asphalt and they bounced along the uneven terrain. Joseph

Guarded Desires

glanced in the rearview as an agitated Stephen continually dialed the Agent he'd tried to reach earlier.

"Goddammit," Stephen muttered under his breath.

"No luck, homey?" said Rigo.

Stephen growled. "No. This is looking pretty fucked right now, buddy. You got your weapon ready?"

"Always."

Stephen gave a sharp nod. "Okay, boys. Be prepared for anything out there."

This time when Joseph glanced behind him, he caught Agent Morris' eye. "You got it."

Stephen gave him a slight smile, then tore his gaze away, seemingly to take in the barren surroundings. Joseph rounded an outcrop of large boulders next to a low rise and almost crashed into another Humvee parked in the dirt. Everyone lurched forward as Joseph braked hard.

"The fuck?" Joseph cried out.

He quickly reached for his weapon. Everyone else readied their weapons as well, and Joseph waited for the DEA agents to call the next move.

Stephen leaned forward from the back seat. "PFC Pirelli, you stay here with the vehicle and have it ready in case we need to vacate the area immediately."

Joseph bristled at the command. On the one hand, it made sense. Yet he felt as though Stephen was purposely keeping him out of the action. Like he was protecting him or something.

Or he could be afraid I'll start shooting at everyone.

"The rest of us are going to examine the other Humvee and begin to investigate, see if we can find anyone—"

"Check it out. It's that asshat, Spender." Rigo pointed to where Joseph assumed Agent Spender was coming from.

Joseph turned to the right where Rigo sat and tracked the direction in which he was pointing. Sure enough, Agent

Spender was strolling toward the Humvee as if he didn't have a care in the world. Joseph buzzed the rear window down on that side as the man approached, but still kept the vehicle running. It seemed odd that none of the several Guardsmen or any other agents were about.

Spender leaned in with one arm resting on the door sill. "What are you jokers doing here? You do realize the Lieutenant assigned this location to me, right? This is *my* operation."

Joseph watched Stephen in the mirror and could tell by the way he clenched his jaw and furrowed his brow that he was not happy with this guy.

"I know what the Lieutenant said," Stephen gritted out. "This isn't about that. Where are your other men?"

"Don't worry about it. That's my problem."

Stephen acted as though he was about to launch himself across Agent Gonzalez to attack Spender, but Rigo blocked him with his arm.

"Whoa there, pardner, let's all take a breath here." Rigo narrowed his eyes at Stephen then regarded Spender. "We were concerned because you weren't picking up and Sanchez at the command post couldn't get hold of his guys either. Are all the Guardsmen with the border agents?"

"Yeah." Spender shrugged. "They were all supposed to pair up and hit several of the areas where the suspected new tunnel construction is. I don't know about Sanchez's guys, but I saw who was calling on my cell ID and had no interest in speaking with you. I *don't* need your help."

"Listen, Spender," Stephen gritted out. "I don't give a shit about your agenda right now. We were fired on back at our position, and the guy who did it came through one of the tunnels.

Spender shrugged again. "Yeah? So?"

Guarded Desires

Stephen pinched the bridge of his nose before responding. "He seemed to already know I was there. It was like he'd targeted me before he ever even exited the tunnel."

"I don't see how that—"

Repeating gunfire sounded off in the distance.

Spender straightened, and Joseph switched off the Humvee's headlights. He swiftly reached into the bag of gear next to him for his night vision goggles then put them on. Spender leaned in to speak in his radio.

A gunshot exploded nearby, splattering the inside of the truck with pieces of Spender's head. Alex cried out as they all crouched lower. Joseph threw the Humvee into reverse, intent on getting to cover so they could assess the situation better. First, they would defend themselves. Then they would attempt to locate their fellow agents and Guardsmen.

Suddenly, they were all immersed in a possible gun battle right on American soil.

Chapter Four

Stephen held on to the door handle as Joseph gunned the vehicle in reverse, prepared to leap from the truck if necessary. As soon as the Humvee was positioned horizontally by the rocks and the other side of the rise, Joseph shut it down. Joseph twisted around, facing Stephen, and he could see the determination in the young man's eyes.

"I'm taking Private Yuen out behind the rocks. We'll have night vision to try and ascertain where the threat is coming from. You guys stay here. You can use the doors as shields and protect our flanks."

"Jesus. Listen to the kid over here," Rigo grumbled.

"I don't like it." Stephen stared him down. "We're completely unprepared for this scenario. We have no way of communicating with you both once you're out there and we're in here. I don't like you being bait for them."

"There's no choice. We can't just sit here and wait for them to ambush us."

Another burst of gunfire broke the silence. Joseph and Stephen held each other's gaze for a moment. He knew Joseph

Guarded Desires

was right, but he was terrified for him after everything that had already gone down that night.

"Dammit. Fine, Pirelli. But as soon as you have anything, get back here so we can decide on our next move."

Joseph nodded and moved to exit the vehicle. Stephen grabbed his arm. "No chasing crazed gunmen across the desert anymore, got it?"

He seemed to be holding a smile at bay as he held Stephen's gaze. "Got it."

Joseph grabbed his M16, and other gear then exited the vehicle, but Stephen noted that Private Yuen was still rooted to his spot in the front seat. Stephen placed a hand on his shoulder and Yuen startled.

"Soldier. You need to get out there with PFC Pirelli."

The kid didn't move, he just continued to stare forward.

"Private Yuen. Your partner is out there alone. Let's get a move on."

Yuen remained frozen. "There wasn't supposed to be real battles. That's why I enlisted in the Guard. My buddies all said it would be easy, I'd get decent pay. They said I wouldn't get deployed for anything other than hurricanes and shit, that there wasn't anything big going down right now—that they didn't need extra troops in Afghanistan or anything like that."

Shit.

Stephen couldn't leave Joseph out there alone. Then he truly would be bait.

"Give me your goggles."

Private Yuen appeared confused. Stephen leaned over the front seat and grabbed the young man's pack. He dragged it back over and set it between him and Rigo.

"What's our move now, homey?"

Stephen dug around inside the bag. "You hold things down

here, and I'll go scout the territory with Joseph. The rest of the plan stays the same."

"You think our guys are still out there?"

"I'm betting on it. The gunfire we've been hearing must be them battling it out. Call Sanchez and let him know what's up. Hopefully the CO is there by now. Maybe he can pull in some more Guardsmen from the armory and send them our way."

"Be careful, man."

"Oh you know it, Gonzalez. There've been too many close calls already."

With the goggles in one hand and his revolver in the other, Stephen dropped to the ground from the truck, keeping low. He crept quickly to the rocks where Joseph had headed. Joseph was flat on his belly, goggles on, peering through a small opening between two boulders. Stephen laid down next to him, his khakis preventing the bigger rocks from digging too sharply into his skin.

Without turning, Joseph growled, "Finally, Yuen. What the hell were you—?"

"Yuen's back at the Humvee."

Joseph whipped his head around, the end of the long lenses of the heavy goggles whacking the side of the rock.

"Ah, shit."

Stephen marveled that Joseph had the presence of mind to keep his voice down even though he'd been surprised.

"What happened to Yuen?"

"Not sure. He's having a panic attack or something. Gonzalez is with him. We can worry about that later. How are things here?"

Joseph pushed the goggles up onto his head. The scowl on his face said it all in terms of how he felt about Private Yuen.

"There's been no movement. Some stray gunfire, but it seems as though it's moving away from us. We need to find the men in my unit as well as the other agents. I'm gonna move in farther and check it out."

"You're aware that your orders are to back up the DEA and CBP, right?"

Joseph cleared his throat and dropped his gaze. "Sorry, sir." He lifted his eyes. "Of course. Whatever you think is the best course of action. We'll... Well, I'll back you up on whatever you decide."

"I think we should find your men and the other agents by moving in farther and checking it out."

Joseph's mouth made a small 'o'. Stephen allowed himself a smile in response. He was rewarded with one back.

"Yes, sir."

They both took one more look at their surroundings with the goggles to verify they were clear. The military grade glasses were more sophisticated than any Stephen had used before, so Joseph had to show him how to adjust the lenses. They were close enough that Stephen could sense the heat from Joseph's body in the cool night air. Joseph had the clean scent of soap mixed with the sweat from the past few hours of insanity.

Once they were able to clear the area, they headed back to the Humvee. Stephen noted that Joseph didn't even acknowledge Private Yuen when he got in the truck. It was the right call. In the heat of things, they didn't have time to get into it with the soldier.

Stephen regarded Rigo. "Get a hold of Sanchez?"

"Yeah. They have us and the rest of the Humvees on GPS. Helicopters will be here in a few, and a caravan of more Humvees should arrive in about forty-five to an hour. They're treating it as a full engagement. They've requested we hold our positions until reinforcements arrive."

Joseph slapped the steering wheel of the truck with both hands. Stephen clasped Joseph's shoulder. "I know. I wanted to move in too." He let go and slumped back in his seat. "All right, men. I guess we sit tight then. Let's stay alert just in case."

Joseph opened the door, then stepped out of the vehicle. Stephen jerked up.

"Where are you going?"

"I'm not going to sit here in this truck and do nothing."

"You can't go against orders."

"I won't. I'm going back in position with the goggles to make sure no one gets the jump on us until help arrives."

Stephen nodded. "Good call. Then I'll go with you. Except you might need to show me how to use these things again."

Joseph chuckled. "They teach you anything at Quantico?"

"That was ten years ago, kid. We were still using cans with string."

Joseph gave him a big smile and shook his head. Stephen loved the dichotomy between the young man's serious side and his playful side. Every small interaction with Joseph added to Stephen's resolve to try and get to know him better.

With any luck, a *lot* better.

Once the reinforcements arrived, and a sweep from air and ground had been completed, it appeared that the threat had passed. Unfortunately, in addition to Agent Spender, two border agents and one of the Guardsmen had lost their lives. There were some additional non-life-threatening injuries to other agents and Guardsmen as well. The entire situation was a nightmare.

Joseph could tell how upset Stephen was by the events that had taken place. It took every ounce of Joseph's resolve not to try and comfort Stephen. He wanted to be near him—even if it was only to stand next to him and nothing more. But with the

Guarded Desires

melee of different agencies milling about, all Joseph was able to do was exchange glances and a smile before heading toward the Humvee.

The time had come to take the vehicle and his sorry ass back to the armory and face the retribution for his earlier actions.

Stephen surprised him by holding up a finger as if to ask him to wait then excused himself from the people he was speaking with. Joseph leaned against the driver's side door, his heart thudding as Stephen approached.

"I want to thank you again, Joseph. For everything. You handled yourself remarkably well out there at the other location, too. The Guard should be very proud to have you representing them. I'm going to stand up for you, don't worry."

Joseph ducked his head, heat filling his cheeks. "Thanks." He lifted his eyes. "I want you to know I'd do it again in a heartbeat."

Joseph also wanted to tell him he'd see him later but had no idea if that would ever be possible. However, his heart soared at Stephen's words. It meant a lot that a seasoned DEA agent had said those things to him. And even more that Stephen—the *man*—had said them.

* * *

Agent Morris' house was located at the end of a long street. Joseph was slowly making his way from the bus stop around the corner, which gave him time to ponder the impulsiveness of his decision to accept Stephen's invitation.

Not Stephen. Agent Morris.

With as hard as he'd been trying to depersonalize the agent who'd become his go-to jack off fantasy, attending a barbeque at the man's house seemed incredibly stupid.

I'm having a cheeseburger and a beer, then I'll leave. No big deal. Plus, there'll be tons of other people there. He probably won't even notice me.

Joseph reasoned that it was the polite thing to do after all that had gone down the other night at the border. It didn't seem necessary to make such a big deal out of it. He'd merely been doing his job. Except that the man he'd saved also happened to be his personal dream guy.

So much had happened in the past few days. The situation at the border was so intense that the proceedings had been sped up regarding the shooting. As promised, Agent Morris had stood up for him when it was time to give a statement. The vehemence with which he'd spoken made it clear that he was only alive because of Joseph's quick thinking.

Right after the proceedings adjourned and Stephen was getting ready to leave, he'd pulled Joseph aside and invited him to the barbeque. Stephen insisted that it was his and Rigo's way of unwinding from the stress of the job, and there would be other agents from their field office attending. Apparently, several of them wanted to meet Joseph to thank him for saving the life of one of their own.

Joseph hadn't been sure how to take the invitation, but he told himself it was nothing more than Agent Morris being nice after all that had happened.

As he strolled up the walkway to Agent Morris' home, laughter and conversation mixed with mariachi music drifted from the house. The screen door was the only thing between him and the inside of Stephen's place. Joseph peered through the screen, his eyes adjusting to the darker interior. He didn't want to barge in unannounced, but at the same time, he doubted anyone would hear him knocking on the thin aluminum frame of the door.

Guarded Desires

While he stood there pondering his next move, he spotted Stephen and Rigo arguing over by the speaker system.

"We've been playing your jam for the past hour. Give your iPod a rest. I have my party mix right here."

Rigo rolled his eyes. "Homey, you do realize this isn't the eighties anymore, right? And the iPod never rests. However, those shiny round discs look as if they could use a nap."

Stephen crossed his arms. "What's wrong with the eighties? Or CDs? This is awesome dance music. I have the Pet Shop Boys, Depeche Mode, Bananarama—"

"Banana what? Don't you dare touch my tunes. Mariachi is *real* dance music."

Joseph couldn't take it any longer. He opened the screen door and stepped inside. "I like the Pet Shop Boys."

Both agents turned his way and froze, still hunched over a dark heavy wood entertainment center. Rigo raised his eyebrows, glanced sideways at Stephen then straightened.

"I guess I'm outvoted. You two enjoy the Pet Shop Guys or whatever they're called. I have some *fajitas* to grill up."

Stephen stood tall, his massive frame made even more alluring in a tight T-shirt and jeans. Joseph swallowed hard.

God help me.

Advancing with his hand held out, Stephen spoke. "I'm really glad you could make it."

Joseph paused for a second before accepting Stephen's handshake. He'd only been there for a little over a minute and already he was touching the man. The agent's firm grip threatened to derail his composure, so Joseph attempted to focus on the safe topics of conversation he'd practiced earlier.

Letting go of Stephen regretfully, he gave him the six-pack of soda he'd brought. He hadn't thought it would be such a good idea to carry beer on the bus. Stephen chuckled.

"Didn't want to be caught with Bud Ice out on the streets of Nogales?"

"It's actually Tecate."

Stephen smirked, eyeing Joseph in a way that sent blood rushing to his groin.

Joseph glanced away to break the moment. When he turned back, Stephen's expression hadn't changed. Joseph swallowed again, trying to regain control of himself.

"How's your knee?"

Polite. Not too personal.

"Happy to still be attached to a living, breathing body."

"I'm happy too." Heat flushed Joseph's face. "I mean, you know, because the alternative would've really sucked."

I should just go home before this gets any worse.

"No joke. But let's forget about all that shit for now and enjoy ourselves." Stephen put his hand on Joseph's shoulder, as if directing him out of the room. Before he could stop himself, Joseph tensed. Stephen furrowed his brow and dropped his hand.

Joseph attempted to salvage the moment by giving him a little smile. Already things were becoming awkward. If only he could relax and relish the chance to spend some free time with Stephen. Would he ever be capable of doing such a thing? He wasn't so sure. But damn, how he wished he could.

* * *

So far, Stephen felt the barbeque had been going well. The sun was lowering on the horizon and soon it would be twilight. Several people had left, and it was now just Rigo, his family and Joseph. It had been near impossible to keep from staring at Joseph all day, but he was proud at how well he'd controlled himself.

For the most part.

There were a couple of times he was sure Joseph had been gazing his way too, but the kid was pretty stealthy. Stephen mused that right from the very first time at the bar there had been quick bursts of connection. Little sparks.

Stephen hoped that being in a social setting with no other pressures would open the door to the possibility of something more. Joseph hadn't made any excuses to leave but he'd also avoided getting too close to Stephen all day.

"Hey homey, come here. I want to show you something." Rigo called to him from inside the sliding glass door.

"I've seen it already and I told you before. I'm not impressed."

Stephen took the last swallow of his beer.

I gotta watch it. I think that was my fifth or sixth.

Two or three was his usual limit but they'd all been hanging out—grilling, eating and joking for almost four hours. He'd also really wanted to unwind more than ever after all the crap he'd been through that week. Stephen glanced Joseph's way, where he was busy chasing Rigo's two boys—eleven and fourteen years old—around with a football. They tossed it back and forth, laughing, obviously having a great time. Rigo's wife Carla winked at Stephen.

"I'm sure it must be very important."

Stephen laughed. "Undoubtedly. Can I get you anything while I'm inside?"

"Thanks, but we're probably going to take off here in a few."

After stacking some plates and cups that were still left outside, Stephen headed into the kitchen from the sliding glass door off the patio. He sighed as he placed the additional dishes in the sink the best he could. Stuff overflowed everywhere onto the counter.

Rigo appeared from the guest bathroom, zipping up his fly as he entered the kitchen.

"I told you. I've seen that already. Once was enough."

"Har har." Rigo looked uncomfortable all of a sudden. "Um, I need to ask you something."

Stephen frowned. Rigo rarely became serious when they weren't on the job. "Yeah, what is it?"

"Is there something going on between you and that kid?"

Stephen hadn't considered that anyone else could tell there was an attraction between them. Well, at least that *he* felt an attraction. He was still unsure what Joseph might be thinking or feeling. But he was damn sure it wasn't any of Rigo's business one way or the other.

"Why are you asking?" Stephen knew his tone had come out a tad harsher than he'd anticipated.

"Don't get ruffled. It's none of my concern—"

"Fuckin' right it isn't."

"Whoa." Rigo held out his palms. "Listen for a sec. The only reason I brought it up is in case there are any further inquiries into what happened out in the desert the other night."

Stephen frowned. "Joseph said that had all been decided already, that there weren't going to be any major repercussions. I don't see how it would affect us in any way now."

"Oh, okay." Rigo nodded. "I suppose that answers all my questions. But that's good. What was the outcome for Joseph? If you don't mind me asking."

"When I go back to the Mesa Armory I'll be suspended from any active or non-active duty operations for sixty days without pay."

Rigo jumped and they both whirled around to see Joseph coming in from outside, several empty beer bottles in his hands.

"Jesus, kid. You're like a ninja." Rigo held a hand over his heart.

Guarded Desires

"Sorry." Joseph had a bit of a lop-sided smile and Stephen was worried about how much he'd actually heard of the conversation. Then he considered what Joseph said.

"Sixty days? You never told me that part. That's bullshit."

Rage built inside Stephen. He wanted to go and talk some sense into whomever it was who'd decided to punish this brave and wonderful man.

Joseph shrugged. "It's okay. It could've been much worse. It all came down to there not being any precedent for what happened. There were some scary moments where it looked as though there was going to be a Court Martial since we're here under Executive Order. Thankfully, they rushed a non-judicial hearing through instead because of how volatile the situation still is at the border. But your statement made a huge difference. I'm really grateful."

Rigo grunted. "See? Your statement made the difference."

Stephen pursed his lips and scowled at Rigo. "It also happened to be the God's honest truth."

"I'm not saying it wasn't. Just that sometimes things can get misinterpreted."

Stephen flipped the bird to no one in general. "They can misinterpret this."

Joseph cleared his throat, drawing the two men's attention. "Did I miss something?"

Stephen stared Rigo down. "The kid wants to know. Did he miss something?"

Rigo held up his hands as if in surrender. "Nah. Nothing's been missed. Especially that eighties dance crap you had on earlier."

"I thought you had a house of your own that you lived in? It's probably *missing* you real bad right now."

Rigo grunted. "Not half as much as *I'm* missing it, trust me.

Let me grab my woman and those two boys who insist on living with us, and we'll all vacate the premises."

"Excellent. I have some Flock of Seagulls I was just getting ready to play."

Rigo jetted out of the patio door yelling, "Carla, kids! Let's go!"

* * *

Joseph went outside to clean up some more while Stephen said his goodbyes to Rigo and his family. He'd stayed at Stephens place way past the time when he'd be able to get a bus to the housing unit he was in. Even though he was off-duty, he didn't want to explain where he'd been so long to anyone—especially if he stayed out late.

Or all night.

He sighed. That wasn't happening. Not even if Stephen was interested. Joseph sensed he was after hearing a little of what Stephen and his partner had been discussing when he'd walked in on them from outside.

And now he could only blame himself. There were several times during the day where he'd thought he had an out, an excuse to leave—then something had held him back. It almost seemed as though Stephen could tell when Joseph was about to bolt.

"Can you help me cut up some tomatoes for the burgers?" or *"I have some more beer in the fridge out in the garage, you mind grabbing that for me?"*

Stephen had never let him out of his sight. And truthfully? He loved it. Joseph ached the hunky bear to want him—to treat him as if he were special and worth loving. Not as if he deserved nothing more than a slap across the face, being whipped with a belt buckle or burned by a lit cigarette ground

Guarded Desires

into his skin. Stephen would cherish him, be protective and want the best for him.

Shut up. You barely know the guy. He could destroy you if he ever got too angry.

Joseph had made himself stronger, he *was* stronger. But he'd never have the sheer brute strength of a man like Stephen. No matter how much he liked Stephen, desired him, thought they'd be good together—he couldn't take the chance. He'd help Stephen clean up some more, be polite, then get the hell out of there.

Stephen stepped outside, regarding him with a warm smile. "You don't have to do all that. I promise I didn't invite you over to be my servant." Stephen chuckled. "I've been ordering you around all day."

Joseph turned to the gorgeous form of Stephen, the man he could never allow himself to have, and gave him a smile back—although, he hadn't been able to put much enthusiasm into it.

"That's okay. It's part of my job description. I'm used to it."

An odd expression passed over Stephen's face, and Joseph wondered what was going on inside his head.

"Everything all right, Joseph?"

That gave him pause. He was certain that Stephen had never said his name before. It had been 'kid', 'Pirelli'—but not Joseph.

He glanced away. His heart raced, his palms clammy and sweaty. Joseph rubbed his hands together, fruitlessly attempting to dry them, gazing around the nice, tidy yard.

It featured a small patch of grass that must be a bitch to keep going in the summer. The back area was all dirt where he'd played with Rigo's boys. A ten by twelve cement foundation at the base of the kitchen steps outside the sliding door held the grill and a four-chair outdoor set. Two redwood benches edged the patio, with terracotta pots filled with varying cacti at the ends of each one. It epitomized the feeling of home.

If only.

He cleared his throat. "Everything's fine. And I don't mind helping."

Joseph purposely glanced down as he gathered the remnants of trash and discarded cans and bottles. The sensation that Stephen eyed his every move was something he couldn't shake. He didn't dare check to see if Stephen actually *was* watching—all resolve would give away otherwise.

I have to get the fuck out of here.

Joseph set the items he'd brought in down on the white-tiled counter. He turned to ask Stephen a question. "Do you have a recycling—?"

Joseph's breath caught in his throat. Stephen was right there. Right in front of him. So close that if either of them moved forward in the slightest, their belt buckles would clang together.

This time, Joseph couldn't tear his gaze away. Stephen stared down at him, his hazel eyes filled with promise. The bulk of the gorgeous man intimidated and aroused him all at the same time.

Lifting only one hand, Stephen brought it slowly to Joseph's cheek and let it rest there. Swallowing hard, Joseph barely managed to keep from flinching. He noted the flicker of concern in Stephen's expression, the golden flecks of his irises suddenly very predominant.

Do they change color with his moods?

It was an odd thought, but he didn't know how to respond to a touch so gentle. It was foreign, almost scary. Joseph pressed his lips together, suddenly terrified that Stephen would try to kiss him. Simultaneously, he was sure he would die if Stephen

Guarded Desires

didn't. The agent stroked his cheek with his thumb, soft and slow.

"I know you've been through a lot already for someone so young. But if you like me even a fraction as much as I like you, I was hoping you might want us to get to know one another better. I would never hurt you."

Could he? Was there any room inside him for trust?

"I...I want to. I mean, get to know each other."

Stephen bent his head and Joseph realized too late that he meant to kiss him. Thin, strong lips captured his and Stephen softly prodded Joseph's mouth open, sliding his tongue inside. Soothing caresses swept through his mouth, and the kiss deepened as Stephen slid a muscled arm around Joseph's waist, pulling him close.

Stephen tightened his embrace and adrenaline shot through Joseph. He pushed at Stephen's broad shoulders, panic taking hold.

Too strong.

Taking a step forward, Stephen completely blocked him in, trapping him against the counter. Joseph squirmed in Stephen's hold, breaking the kiss.

"No!"

Stephen jumped back, dropping his arms. Joseph's breathing came in frantic gasps, his body shaking. He lifted his gaze and Stephen appeared as if he were in pain.

"I'm so sorry, Joseph. I thought you..." He winced and shook his head. "I must've misunderstood."

Closing his eyes, Joseph willed himself to calm down. The brief moment that Stephen held and kissed him had been sweeter and more wonderful than any physical interaction he'd ever had.

And I fucked it up.

Joseph opened his eyes, lifting his gaze to meet Stephen's. He'd moved even farther back and was no longer within reach.

"You didn't misunderstand." Joseph dragged a still shaky hand over the top of his head. "But I have to go."

He briskly made his way through the living room, and once he'd pushed the screen door open, jogged down the street as fast as he could. He barely heard Stephen yelling out for him to wait, that he would give him a ride. But he didn't stop, didn't dare look over his shoulder.

He didn't trust himself any more than he trusted Stephen.

Chapter Five

"**H**ey, Pirelli! Where the fuck you been?"

Great. Barnett.

Joseph ignored him as he continued down the long hallway to his room.

"Pirelli! I was fucking talking to you. If you're in a hurry to get to your boyfriend Yuen, he's long gone."

Joseph halted. He didn't bother contemplating the boyfriend remark. He was more concerned with what Barnett meant by Alex being long gone. Joseph turned to face Barnett the Missing Link.

"What do you mean, gone?"

Barnett crossed his arms, leaning against the wall with a smirk. "You know—Gone. As in *left*. And we sure been hearing a lotta interesting stuff around here. See, one of Griffin's best buddies works in the office at the armory. He mentioned there was much more to your whole hero in the desert story than was originally told."

"I never talked about anything with anyone..."

Barnett snorted. "Exactly. Which is why we had to find our

own sources to get to the bottom of this whole thing." He sniggered. "So to speak."

"What does any of this have to do with Yuen?"

The heat of anger built inside him. He was frustrated, sad and horny from the encounter with Stephen, and now this baboon was intent on baiting him.

Barnett held onto his lop-sided, sneering grin. "Everyone here has pretty much guessed the reason why Yuen was discharged from this mission."

"Discharged? But I thought..." Joseph didn't want to say any more. It could all be a ruse to get him to blab about Alex's personal business. From the way he'd understood things, it had been left that Alex wouldn't go out on any more field missions for the remainder of their Active Duty at the border. However, Joseph hadn't been sure about anything more than that in terms of long-term repercussions.

Barnett raised his eyebrows. "Yeah? What did you think, huh? Sad your boyfriend left you?"

An aggravated sigh fell from his lips. Clearly, his sexual orientation had been revealed. The field reports detailed his statements regarding his ex, and how he'd known the deceased. One of Barnett and Griffin's grimy friends had spouted off about things that should have been kept under wraps. Not that he could ever prove anything.

Whatever. It's only a couple more weeks.

He fixed Barnett with a steely glare. "Nah, I'm not upset. I'd already broken up with him anyway."

Joseph turned on his heels and marched toward his door, ignoring a string of gay slurs being hurled his way. After closing himself up in his now single occupancy room, he threw himself on his bed.

He'd known that Alex would have to answer for crapping out on them out there, as rightly he should. When others were

Guarded Desires

relying on a soldier's ability to perform under pressure, and that soldier unable to keep it together, it could cost people their lives.

However, he'd held out hope that there would be a way for them to continue working together and that Alex would get a chance to prove himself again. Also, as much as Alex had been annoying at times, he was the only recruit at Nogales that Joseph felt even a little comfortable with.

And now he was stuck with two guys who would be harassing him constantly and one man he would be thinking about endlessly.

* * *

I really fucked that up good.

Stephen was sprawled across his sofa, one arm behind his head, his thoughts in a whirl as he tried to force himself to relax. Despite being as horny as hell, Stephen didn't feel like getting himself off. There had been such a sweet moment between him and Joseph in the kitchen, and he'd destroyed it by being too eager.

Even before he'd heard about Joseph's abusive relationship with Dorian, he'd discerned there was something the young man was protecting himself from. Somehow, the relaxing day they'd shared and Joseph admitting that he'd like to get to know him better too, had made Stephen think he could at least kiss and hold him.

He honestly hadn't expected anything more from Joseph. Everything was overwhelming because of their positions, age difference and Joseph's past, so he'd assumed they would move slowly. Now it seemed that Joseph might not want to move at all.

The kitchen had been cleaned meticulously—every dish,

cup and utensil washed, counters wiped clean, hell—even the grill had been scrubbed down. Now it was after midnight and there wasn't the slightest chance he'd be getting to sleep any time soon.

Yup. Fucked up is right.

The situation with Joseph was too much to deal with for the time being anyway. He had a particularly difficult and troubling case to work on and every ounce of his energy should be spent focusing on that and not his dick. Plus, even though the kid was smart, beautiful and sexy, he was also very young and had been through a lot of trauma. It probably wouldn't be the most brilliant thing in the world to get involved with him.

Resigning himself to continued loneliness for a while, Stephen shut off the TV, and pushed up from the couch. It was time to force himself to go lie down in his empty bed.

* * *

"Jesus, Stephen. How many beers did you have last night?"

A mopey and exhausted Stephen glared at Rigo before he sat down at his desk, which was placed opposite his partner's. "It wasn't the beers."

Rigo raised his eyebrows. "Oh?" He leaned forward and lowered his voice. "You and the kid do the horizontal mambo all night then?"

Stephen dropped his head into his hands.

Why me?

He looked up and considered Rigo. What was his partner getting at exactly? Stephen's expression must've been telling.

Rigo frowned. "Quit looking at me like that. I'm not being critical. About other things, sure—I mean how many X-Files reruns can a human being tolerate in one lifetime? But as far as you..." Rigo paused as another agent walked, nodding at them before continuing on his way. He turned back to Stephen. "You and that kid goes, I thought it over and you were right."

"Huh?" Stephen tilted his head.

"Remember how Carla and I got together?"

That threw Stephen off, but he recalled that she'd been Rigo's direct supervisor at the police station he'd worked at in Tucson, right after he'd first gotten into law enforcement. They'd been unable to hold themselves back from getting together and when they'd been caught, Carla had almost lost her position. Then, Rigo had been forced to transfer. It was actually how he'd ended up working in the DEA, since he'd needed to choose a completely different department.

"Yeah, I remember. So?"

"You know, originally, I was ecstatic to be partnered with you because you seemed so smart. But now I'm wondering."

"Rigo...not in the mood today."

"Look. I don't need details. As a matter of fact, I prefer that there be no details—or even vague allusions—but obviously something happened between you two last night. I don't know if you guys got together and it was no good, or you didn't get together, or maybe my big mouth ruined things. But what I *do* know is that both of you are obviously into each other, and quite frankly, in the last two years I've never seen that look on your face."

"What look?"

"The one where you gawk at Joseph as if he were better than my mother's chili rellenos. And I didn't think such a thing was possible."

Stephen chuckled. "That obvious?"

"Whatever didn't go right, figure out a way to fix it. Because even though love-sick Agent Morris was getting on my last good nerve, depressed and cranky Agent Morris is much worse. You and Joseph want each other. Bad. Please go do something about it before I have to slap you."

Stephen leaned back in his desk chair, swaying in it slightly as he contemplated Rigo's words. He rested his elbows on the chair arms as he held his hands folded in his lap, tapping the ends of his thumbs together.

Before coming into the office, he'd pretty much decided to let Joseph go and move on with his life. Then Rigo had rocked his world by what he said. Hearing from his good friend that Stephen should take a chance with the young man had his gut churning again. There was hope and desire, but also much uncertainty.

One more try. It couldn't hurt, right?

But first, he had a lot to handle for the day. After going over all that had happened at the border a few nights before, he and Rigo had something they wanted to bring up to Boyd. Stephen was certain his boss wouldn't like it. Boyd was already in a foul mood over everything that had gone down that awful night.

Stephen and Rigo had discussed at length how they felt about everything that happened in the desert. It was unsettling to realize that if they'd gone on the mission the way they'd intended to—it could've been them who lost their lives. And if they combined the fact that it was their investigative work which had led to the deadly mission, it made Stephen more determined than ever to take down the bastards from the cartel.

In their line of work, there were no guarantees. Just as he and Rigo had known of the risks when they signed on, so had Spender. And Stephen was more than happy to head out to the same area and investigate some more, regardless of the danger. But first, they needed to float their theory to Boyd.

Hopefully, their boss wouldn't have a complete meltdown.

* * *

Guarded Desires

Since the night at the border when Joseph had gunned down Dorian's old partner, his CO had kept him on fairly routine operations until it was time for him to take his unpaid leave in Mesa. Nothing had been said about Private Yuen, and Joseph wondered if he would ever find out what had happened to him. So far, no one had been moved into his room. Knowing that it was now likely common knowledge that he was gay, he couldn't help but think that the revelation was why he was rooming alone.

"Pirelli. I don't suppose you have a lighter on you, do you?"

Joseph glanced at Private Harrison. They'd barely spoken before, but Joseph knew the guardsman had been close to getting taken out when everything had gone down in the desert.

They were taking a fifteen-minute break in the shade by the same building Joseph had been interrogated in. Both he and Dan Harrison were pulling regular patrol duty by providing support to the CBP during the day at the Nogales border crossing. Joseph was sure he wouldn't have to worry about running into Agent Morris anymore now that he was stuck pulling day shifts.

"Pirelli? Light?"

"Oh, sorry. Woolgathering. No, I don't smoke."

"Shit. Oh, well. My own damn fault."

Harrison seemed to be muttering more to himself than to Joseph. An awkward pause stretched out between them.

Harrison cleared his throat. "So, I hear you wasted one of them the other night."

Joseph cringed. As the days went by, he'd heard plenty of comments, rumors and whisperings about that night. Almost everyone had seemed to form new opinions regarding him. He'd tried so hard to keep to himself and simply do his job but that was unlikely to work out anymore. No one in his platoon had addressed him directly about what had gone down, unless it was Griffin or Barnett hurling insults at him.

Joseph stared off in the distance. "I don't know as if that's how I'd put it."

"Then how would you put it?"

He didn't know this guy, didn't have an opinion about him one way or the other. But something in his tone didn't come across as challenging or hostile. Harrison seemed genuinely curious.

They were both leaning against the building, about five feet apart, waving idly at the tiny flies that sometimes buzzed around their faces. Joseph glanced sideways, appraising the slightly built, blond-haired man. He was probably one of the new recruits. Maybe even fresh out of high school.

"I was doing my job," answered Joseph. "I happened to have prior knowledge that the guy coming out of the tunnel was a murderer, and I chased after him before he could kill any of our agents. That's all there was to it."

"But the guy you killed used to be your boyfriend, right? That's pretty hardcore."

Joseph almost choked. *That's what everyone thinks?*

He still couldn't detect any malice in Harrison's voice, but Joseph wanted to make damn sure he had the story straight.

"That guy was most definitely *not* my boyfriend."

"I see." Harrison let out a long sigh. "You're going to pretend you're not gay. Great. I thought maybe there was *someone* I could talk to."

"Excuse me? I never said I wasn't gay, only that I was never with that piece of shit." Joseph latched onto what else Harrison had said. "Whaddya mean you thought you had someone you could talk to?"

Harrison furrowed his brow. "So...you *are* gay?"

Joseph groaned. "Why is everyone so fucking fascinated by

my orientation? I don't go around all day saying 'Oh my God, I wonder if he's straight? How can we ask him without him getting offended?' Get over it already."

"I know, right?"

The fuck?

"Harrison, are you trying to tell me something?"

"Well, yeah. I mean, I'm gay too." He cringed.

"Jesus, don't hurt yourself by saying it out loud."

Harrison lowered his head and Joseph couldn't tell if he was angry, upset or sad.

"You don't have to be mean. I thought you'd understand."

A twinge of remorse hit Joseph in the chest. "Hey, I'm sorry. It's just that I don't know you, and with all the shit that's gone on this week, I guess I got too defensive."

Harrison didn't respond, and Joseph wasn't sure if he should say anything else or leave well enough alone. Then Harrison lifted his head and locked eyes with him.

"I didn't admit to myself that I was gay until a couple months ago. Right before I went into basic."

"Wow. Epic timing on that one."

Harrison snorted. "Yeah. No kidding."

"So... You admitted to yourself and no one else?"

Harrison turned away, squinting against the brightness of the sun-drenched desert. "No. I fucked it up completely by telling my parents, too. I had this idea that I might die or something out here and I didn't want them to think I was someone that I wasn't. Does that sound crazy?"

Joseph shook his head. "No. I think I get it. But you'd just figured it out for yourself, right? What was the defining moment?

Harrison chuckled. "That's just it, there wasn't one." He shrugged. "I'd toyed with the idea that I was probably bisexual for a while. But in the past year, all I've been able to think about are guys, and the more and more I let myself just go with it, the more I realize I've been pretending ever since my first woody that I ever liked girls at all."

Joseph pondered that. He'd never had the deep 'when did I know I was gay' conversation with anyone before.

Harrison regarded Joseph. "What about you? When did you know?"

Joseph snorted. "When I was born and couldn't wait to escape my mom's vagina."

Harrison screwed up his nose. "Dude! Why would you say something like that?"

The horror that blossomed on Harrison's features was so hysterical that Joseph burst out laughing. "Oh my God, you should see your expression!"

"I seriously can't believe you just said that." Then Harrison laughed a little. "But for real, you always knew?"

Joseph nodded. "I don't think there's one certain way people discover their truth, whether they're gay, straight or otherwise. And I don't really think it matters as long as a person is comfortable with who they are."

Harrison nodded. "That's cool. Thanks."

Joseph smiled, feeling better than he had since racing from Stephen like a scared child.

But then the reminder of that night stole his moment of happiness. He'd been wallowing in misery ever since leaving Stephen the way he had. Joseph had played the sweet kiss and strong, comforting embrace over and over in his mind, filled with extreme regret that he'd pushed Stephen away. He was sure Stephen wouldn't want to have anything to do anymore with someone so immature and with so many obvious emotional issues.

Dorian always said that no one else would ever want me

Guarded Desires

except him. He obviously wanted to make sure that was true by fucking with my head the way he did.

Anger boiled beneath the surface of his skin. In the same way that he'd worked so hard to overcome his physical weaknesses, there had to be a way to eliminate his emotional scars—or at least minimize them. He couldn't keep letting Dorian have control over his life almost two years after he'd last seen him. That way, if he ever met anyone as wonderful as Stephen again, he'd be able to accept the goodness that person had to offer instead of pushing them away.

* * *

Stephen figured he could stare at his phone all day, or he could call Joseph. Maybe a text would be less threatening? Or it could be misinterpreted if it wasn't worded perfectly.

Fucking technology.

They had exchanged info the day Stephen came down to make his statement. Because Joseph had completed enough Advanced Individual Training days, he was one of the few men in his unit allowed to have a cell phone or off-duty free time. However, this would be the first time Stephen had used the number.

If he even picks up.

Boyd had scheduled a private rundown of what he and Rigo had come up with in terms of the investigation. Then once Boyd approved the next course of action, there would be a meeting with the entire investigative team to determine their next move. The briefing with his boss was going down in about thirty minutes, so Stephen needed to make his move.

Stephen put down the phone on his cluttered desk. He could call later. What he really needed to do first was to put his game face on. Glancing up, he spotted Rigo approaching their desks from the entrance, which was about twenty feet away. In each hand were two Starbuck's coffees.

The central area of the Nogales resident office of the DEA was a large square room where the agents worked on their separate investigations. Meeting rooms, a break area, and Boyd's office comprised the rest of the layout at the secretly located building. After setting one of the cups on Stephen's desk, then the other on his own, Rigo plopped down in his chair.

"I got you your Americano. They were all out of the Mexicanos."

"Hilarious. But thanks." Stephen took a noisy sip and set the cup down. They sat in silence, Rigo staring at him until Stephen couldn't stand it any longer.

"What?" He knew his voice sounded irritated. The past week had wreaked havoc with him on all fronts.

"Well? Did you call him?"

"When did you go into the matchmaking business? The pay not enough here? Looking for a side hustle?"

"I was going to, but since you're my first love-sick client, I'm afraid I might fail miserably. Then I'll never get to have my dream career." Rigo crossed his arms with a scowl. "Fucking call him already."

"We have a meeting with Boyd in twenty minutes. I'll do it later."

"Yeah. *Twenty minutes.* Are you planning to read *War and Peace* to him?" Rigo snatched Stephen's coffee off his desk.

"Hey!"

"No more coffee goodness for you until you pry your ass out of that chair and call Joseph."

"You're a weirdo."

"Which would be the only explanation as to why I have you as my partner. Now go!"

Guarded Desires

* * *

Joseph's lunch break was almost over. After having the conversation with Dan earlier, a nice camaraderie had built between them. Harrison was in one of the other houses and Joseph was sorry they couldn't room together so he could have a friend to talk to. He'd never dare bring up that idea since his whole unit knew he was gay. Any guy who got put in his room would be subjected to Barnett and Griffin's harassment.

Of course, he could always file a sexual harassment complaint, but the duration of his time with the two morons would likely be over before he ever got very far. Plus, he had enough to deal with on an official level as it was.

His cell phone buzzed, and he plucked it from his pocket. *Probably mom checking in.*

Joseph hesitated, a flutter in his chest when he saw who it was. For a moment, he considered ignoring the call, but that was really not an option. Even though he knew he should stay away from Stephen, he didn't think he had the strength to resist. Stephen was practically the only thing he'd thought about in days.

Joseph glanced around to make sure he was still alone and that no one looked as though they might be about to come into the small break area.

"Hello?"

Stephen cleared his throat. "Hi, Joseph. Is this a good time?"

Joseph caught himself doing the same thing. "Yeah, it's fine."

"Great."

A pause stretched out and Joseph checked the phone to make sure the call hadn't dropped.

Stephen sighed. "Look, I'm very sorry I came on too strong

the other night. We probably should've sat and talked for a while before anything like that happened."

"I liked it." Joseph cringed. He had a tendency to blurt things out.

"Huh?" Stephen paused again.

Joseph racked his brain for something less goofy to say in follow-up.

Stephen finally broke the silence. "Um, I'm sorry, but I'm a little confused. You ran out of there after pushing me away like I disgusted you and I wouldn't typically classify that as meaning you liked what I was doing." Stephen groaned. "Look, as I said before, I know you've been through some shit, so I don't mean to come off as insensitive here. I was just hoping that maybe you would..." Joseph heard some unintelligible muttering. "...would you want to get together some time and talk? I'd ask Rigo to chaperone us, but he might start hitting on you, and I'd only get jealous. I'd probably even call him some very ugly names. It would make things really awkward for me at work."

Joseph chuckled. He really liked Stephen a lot, and the man was completely different from Dorian in every way besides his body mass. He couldn't let the shit that had happened with his ex and abuser run his life anymore. It was time that he allowed himself a chance at happiness with another man.

"Sure. That would be great."

"It would?"

Joseph laughed a bit harder this time. Stephen had actually sounded shocked.

Stephen continued, "When's your next time off?"

"Not until the weekend. I'll have twenty-four hours beginning Saturday morning at eight o'clock."

Another pause. "Okay. I'm having a meeting here in a few

Guarded Desires

minutes, so I'll call you after that and let you know how things look for me this weekend."

Excitement rushed through him. "Sounds good. Um, I'm going back on duty here in a sec, so just leave a message and I'll call you later, okay?"

"More than okay. And thanks for taking my call, Joseph."

God, I love it when he says my name.

"You're welcome." It sounded silly as soon as he said it out loud. "So, I'll talk to you later then. Bye."

Stephen chuckled. "Until later. Bye, Joseph."

After ending the call, Joseph pondered how he was going to keep from going insane with anticipation until the weekend—and how he was going to keep from ruining everything with Stephen. If he froze up again, he doubted that even the most patient and compassionate of men would want to put up with him.

But the only man he hoped would want him since getting away from Dorian was the hunky bear of an agent. He couldn't fuck it up.

Chapter Six

Special Agent in Charge Boyd had just finished meticulously putting away some papers on his desk while ignoring both Stephen and Rigo. It was a typical Boyd move. He would insist that his agents be ready for him at a moment's notice, then leave them to twiddle their thumbs as he performed some random task. Sometimes Stephen wondered if the man was operating on all cogs.

At last Boyd settled into his desk chair and folded his hands in his lap. He regarded them, a look of seeming concentration on his face. "Gentleman, we have a real problem here."

No shit, Sherlock.

Boyd continued. "I'm afraid I won't be able to cover for you guys much longer if you don't start getting some real results. Not only that, but all those men losing their lives on a mission that was based on intelligence the both of you presented is concerning, to say the least." He shrugged. "Of course, *I* would never think this, but it might almost seem like a set-up. That maybe you wanted to send all those guys out there to get picked off."

Guarded Desires

"*Excuse* me?"

Rigo grabbed Stephen's forearm, squeezing hard.

"Well, you have to admit it could look that way. I mean, you were both so adamant there was solid evidence that construction on tunnels was going on."

"So?" Stephen could barely control his seething rage. His face was flushed with heat, and his breathing had sped up. In addition, Rigo's grip on his arm was getting tighter and tighter. "How does that equate to a set-up, huh? I don't remember stating in our report that only cute and cuddly drug smugglers would be coming out of the tunnels." Stephen turned to a wide-eyed Rigo. "What about you, Rigo? Did you misinterpret the field operation as being a perfectly safe mission that we could probably take all of our grandmothers on?" Stephen leaned over the desk and glared at Boyd. "And another thing—"

"Homey, don't."

Rigo gritted the statement through his teeth, but Stephen shrugged off his hold and continued. "I distinctly remember you being the one who insisted that Spender go on that mission. Rigo and I wanted to be the ones to take the lead there—it was our work. Not only *that*, but we have no way of knowing exactly what he was doing out there before everything went to hell. When we first pulled up, he was strolling around like he was on a grand vacation."

Boyd favored Stephen with a steady gaze, his hands clasped behind his head and leaning back in his desk chair as if they were deciding on what to order for lunch. It seemed as though nothing could rattle the guy.

"I understand your frustration, Agent Morris. However, we need to take everything into consideration, look at it from all angles. It would be remiss of me not to alert you to any and all situations that could impact your careers and future."

Stephen didn't buy it. And now that he'd spouted off, he

Morticia Knight

was certain that it hadn't helped him or Rigo out in the slightest. But at least there was a good chance that he wouldn't completely implode in Boyd's office—he'd had to vent.

Boyd checked his pricey wristwatch. "Now that we have that out of the way, I do want to hear your new theory. We have a general briefing here in a bit and I need to determine our next move. Gentlemen, what do you have for me?"

Since Stephen was certain he'd just been crossed off Boyd's Christmas list, he wasn't sure if he should be the one to present what he and Rigo believed was going on. Even without his outburst, it would likely piss Boyd off.

"Rigo?" Stephen wanted his partner to have the option on which one of them should lay their theory out.

Rigo regarded Stephen with narrowed eyes. "Please. Allow me." Rigo turned to Boyd. "Essentially, sir, what we're looking at here are episodes that originally seemed unrelated, but in light of what happened the other night, Agent Morris and I now believe they are all connected.

"When I went to make that drug buy the other day, everything was completely fine up until that point in time. Not only was it obvious that they already knew I was an agent from the second I set foot out of the car, but they'd made a concerted effort to get me out in a remote area all alone.

Rigo shook his head. "Then you look at the incident where Agent Morris almost lost his life. The statement from the Guardsman was how it seemed as though the deceased knew where Stephen was. You add that to the fact that the only people who knew Spender and his team were at a previously uncharted location were this office, the Guard and CBP, and there is only one obvious conclusion." Rigo let out a loud exhale. "We have at least one mole, possibly more."

As was typical, the man once again leaned back in his chair, assuming his 'deep in thought' pose. Stephen couldn't help but

Guarded Desires

steal a glance at Rigo, but his partner maintained his placid stare, as if being careful to avoid making eye contact with him.

Boyd leaned forward and folded his hands on his desk. "I suppose that's a possibility, so now we need to be extra aware."

Right. Because we've been such slackers this whole time.

"I'm going to keep the both of you out there in the desert where the new tunnels seem to be. Our agency will get together with the CBP and make sure their agents aren't out there alone anymore until we can figure out this mess. Of course, we're going to need as much support from the Guard as possible."

Joseph. Will they send him back out?

It was ridiculous to think that way about a military man, nor was it that he perceived Joseph as being weak. He simply didn't want the young man to be where the danger was.

Boyd cracked his knuckles. "I'm going to have the rest of the men check out leads plus drag in any and all dealers and users that we know of—no matter how inconsequential they seem. I need to get a handle on this son of a bitch of a case. I'm counting on you both."

"Yes, sir, we're on it."

Stephen let Rigo answer for them, he had nothing else to say to Boyd. At least nothing that wouldn't get him fired.

* * *

Stephen tripped over his own feet unlocking his front door, cursing as he grabbed the jamb. He was rewarded with a brutal splinter for his efforts.

Now I'm awake.

After pulling all-nighters out in the field the last few days, he was pretty worn out, his sleep schedule all jacked up. It had been disturbingly quiet in the desert too. Operating on his usual gut instinct, it seemed as though they were missing something—that maybe the whole assignment at that locale was turning into a complete waste of time.

Maybe the cartel knows better now and is reconsidering their efforts in that section. Maybe last week was just a horrible coincidence.

He knew that was bullshit. In addition, the sophistication of the tunnel that Antonio had emerged from spoke of an incredibly well-funded and elaborate operation. It was hardly the work of a small, unskilled group. After investing that much effort into building tunnels that the agents still couldn't locate, the cartel should be out there rabidly protecting them.

But if we do have a mole...

Stephen was much too exhausted to keep contemplating the various scenarios. He checked his watch, and noting it was almost nine a.m. As soon as he found out what his schedule was like, he'd called Joseph. The plan was for him to come by at five p.m. so that Stephen would have a chance to sleep for a few hours.

At first, Joseph had hesitated a little when Stephen suggested they meet back at his house again, but the reality was that neither of them thought it would be a good idea to go out in public until things cooled down. Or until they'd figured out what they were—or might be—to each other.

Stephen stripped off his filthy, dust-covered clothes, then stepped into the shower. He hadn't been able to keep to his usual workout routine in the last couple of weeks and that was messing with his ability to unwind. His intensive training not only kept his body in the shape he preferred, but it also helped him to work off a lot of stress.

Rolling around on the bed with Joseph would probably help with that too.

His cock filled at the thought of being entwined with Joseph's naked body, caressing the hard planes of his lean flesh,

Guarded Desires

tasting his sweet mouth the way he had the previous week. Unconsciously, Stephen fisted his lengthening shaft. Using his other hand to support himself against the shower wall, he continued his fantasy of Joseph.

The next scene in his head was the beautiful young man with the soulful eyes servicing Stephen with his lips and tongue. Stephen would be lying back on the bed, clutching Joseph's hair, but allowing him to have control. Letting him be in charge so that he wouldn't be afraid of his power being taken away.

Stephen froze, his eyes widening.

That's it.

It wasn't that Joseph didn't want him—it was that Stephen had scared him by trapping him against the counter. Now he had a new quandary. Stephen was an adamant top, a lusty man who liked being the aggressor in sex, loved the way another man would submit to his strength and passion. But he was also a giving and considerate lover. Nothing gave him more joy than seeing the rapture on his partner's face when he brought him to an intense climax.

I'd never hurt him. But will he ever be able to trust me enough to let go?

Stephen straightened, lowering his hand from the wall and releasing his dick. He wasn't sure how comfortable they would be talking over the finer details of intimacy with each other so soon, but the reality was that Joseph's active duty would be completed in a week. Then what?

His exhaustion washed over him again. Sleep was badly needed, then he would do what he always did. Follow his gut. See what happened when he and Joseph got together.

So far, guessing had gotten him nowhere.

* * *

Joseph's fingers trembled a little as he buttoned up his green plaid shirt. He also wore a light wash denim, glad to be in his civvies for a while. He checked himself in the mirror and verified that his face was completely shaved. His hair could've used a bit of a trim, but he hadn't had time to get to the barber at the armory the previous day.

He and Private Harrison pulled duty together a couple of times in the past week, and it had been nice. In addition, Barnett and Griffin were fighting over something stupid that Joseph didn't care about. What he did care about was that it kept the two annoying men off Joseph's back.

He was more relaxed than he'd been since arriving at the border.

Joseph ducked out of the house that held nine recruits from his unit and made his way to the bus stop. He'd quickly nixed the idea of Stephen coming to pick him up. He didn't care what type of altercation Barnett and Griffin were in. If an older hot guy came to get him, he would never hear the end of it. Joseph wanted the night to be something nice, special even.

He knew the reality of their situation. Even if he ignored the obvious age difference, they didn't live and work in the same town. True, it was only a little over three hours between where they lived, but it wasn't the same as being down the street. And he could get deployed at any time—there were no guarantees where that was concerned. Joseph doubted Stephen would want to not only put up with Joseph's emotional crap, but wait around to see if he would even be there at all.

Joseph rubbed his forehead, attempting to ignore the derogatory words running through his brain that Dorian had always hurled at him. Anything the bastard could think of was what he would use against Joseph. In addition to reminding him over and over that no one would ever want him other than Dorian, there were the abusive rants he would spew over and

Guarded Desires

over. Dorian yelled at him that he was weak and useless. That the only thing he would ever be good for was fucking. Otherwise, he was ugly and stupid.

His insane captor had also made sure that other men would think he was ugly by scarring him physically. And Joseph didn't need anyone to tell him he was stupid. He reminded himself of that all the time whenever he thought about how he'd gotten together with Dorian in the first place.

He'd wanted to be one of the cool guys. His life had been endlessly aggravating to have the kids at school shun or tease him. It wasn't as though he didn't have friends or people he could hang out with, it was that they weren't popular. So, when one of the bullies had invited him to a party, Joseph had been surprised and flattered.

He didn't discover until later that when Dorian was doing a drug deal near the school, he'd spotted Joseph on the track field. The invitation had been a way to lure Joseph over to Dorian's home, and before he could stop and think, the next two years of his life were mapped out for him.

Joseph gave himself a mental shake. *That's over. I can't change it. But I can change how I act toward Stephen tonight.*

The bus ride took what amounted to forever in Joseph's anxious mind, even though Stephen's place was probably less than ten miles from the armory. Excitement pooled low in his belly, and he resolved not to behave like a goofy kid once he arrived at Stephen's home.

When the bus pulled up at the correct stop, Joseph rose on shaky legs, the anticipation of seeing Stephen and being alone with him again almost too much to handle.

The last time I was there...

It didn't matter. They were starting fresh.

The spring day wasn't as warm as they'd been recently, and a light wind blew. Even though the breeze wasn't cool, it was nice to feel the air move around a bit. He knew from experience that they only had a few more weeks before summer would strike with a vengeance. But for now, it would be a comfortable evening for him and Stephen to relax and get to know one another a little. Maybe even a lot.

As Joseph strolled up to Stephen's house, he noted that only the closed screen stood between him and the man who had become all he could think about. It was difficult to tell which was the predominant emotion inside him—excitement or fear.

When he reached the entrance, sounds of Stephen banging around in the kitchen reached his ears, so he called out. Stephen appeared at the front door, a happy grin stretching his lips wide. Joseph's stomach fluttered and he swallowed hard. He was glad he'd agreed to come to the agent's house. Even if they couldn't be together the way Joseph truly wished, it was nice to be desired, to have someone so eager to see him—and not because he yearned to punish or abuse him in some way.

"Come in, I was just throwing together some salad. I was thinking we could order a pizza to go with that. Sound good?"

He nodded as Stephen opened the screen and gestured for him to enter.

Joseph willed himself to move and he walked past Stephen, overly conscious of how close they were as he passed him.

"Thanks."

He knew he sounded awkward. Unsure. He was certain his body language telegraphed that as well. As much as he didn't think there would be any long-term prospects for them, that still didn't mean he wanted to be perceived as a scared little kid.

He stopped as soon as he was inside and glanced around the living room. He hadn't really paid much attention to it the last time he'd been there, as they had spent the majority of their time outside. Then there had been the kitchen and he'd run right out of there.

Stephen's house was homey, comfortable. A dark brown fabric sofa and matching love seat were set at an angle and adorned with throw pillows. The wood coffee table was topped with oval glass, and fitness, gun and outdoor magazines were strewn upon it. The entertainment center that Stephen and Rigo had been arguing at was in front of it, and the walls held framed photos of beautiful southwestern vistas, including the Grand Canyon.

"Would you like to have a seat? I can grab us each a beer." Stephen paused and cleared his throat. "I picked up some Bud Lite."

Joseph raised his eyes to acknowledge Stephen, determined to quit acting so shy. "That sounds great, thanks."

Without waiting for a response, Joseph turned away and made his way to the sofa, sitting on the end closest to the kitchen.

"All right, I'll just grab those and be right back."

While there was a slightly nervous edge to Stephen's voice, Joseph could tell he was going out of his way to sound cheery and welcoming.

He's probably worried I'll run out of here again.

Stephen came back with the beers, grabbed two tiled coasters with an Aztec design on them, then placed the beers on top. He took a seat on the sofa as well, but Joseph noted that he was careful to sit in the middle and not too close. They sat in silence, neither one seemingly willing to be the first to speak.

At last, Stephen spoke. "Joseph, I don't want to only make small talk with you, and I didn't ask you to come here so I could get laid..." Joseph peeked up at Stephen, wondering where he was going with the whole conversation. "Of course, if you came over here to lay *me*, then I suppose I could be convinced to give in to your wishes."

Joseph chuckled and was rewarded with a big smile.

"Am I making this too awkward?"

Just hearing the brawny agent sound so vulnerable and unsure of himself calmed Joseph down.

"Very. But that's all right. I've always had a thing for tongue-tied, self-conscious men."

"Ah, a troublemaker I see." Stephen winked. "Before we launch into any deep, soul-baring conversations, you wanna relax a little, eat something and maybe watch a film?"

Joseph let out a relieved sigh. "Actually, that would be fantastic. I haven't kicked back with anyone for a while."

Stephen placed his hands on his knees as if to push himself up. "Done. Favorite type of pizza?"

Stephen stood and Joseph was reminded of what a large man he was. But he also reminded himself that his build was *not* what informed him as a person.

"I'm not that picky. But anything with sausage is always good."

"I'd make some sort of ridiculous joke about that, but I'm trying to behave myself."

Joseph laughed out loud, and it struck him how much he enjoyed Stephen's corny and sarcastic humor. The last thing anyone could've accused Dorian of was having a sense of humor.

I can't keep comparing them.

"Why don't you pick out something from my primarily sci-fi and action film collection of DVDs? I do have a few rather crude comedies in there as well, in case you hate sci-fi and action."

Joseph squinted in the direction of Stephen's film collec-

Guarded Desires

tion, glancing at the selections haphazardly piled up on and around the piece of furniture housing the TV.

"Actually, I can already see you have a few of my faves. I'm a big fan of those types of movies."

Stephen broke into a big grin. "Oh good. I was concerned. You know, since you seem like such a rom com fan. There are only so many times I can watch *Pretty Woman*."

Joseph snorted laughter, honestly enjoying himself with Stephen, his heart filling with hope.

Chapter Seven

The credits came up on *Robocop* and Stephen stretched. "Peter Weller just kicks so much ass in that movie. Love it."

"I know. I wish he'd done more of that genre of film over the years."

Stephen nodded. "Agreed. But he was in the *Star Trek* reboot."

"What did you think of him in that?"

"Awesome, but I'm not completely sold on the new franchise. I'm an old school trekkie."

"What about Chris Pine though?"

"Only reason I set foot in the theater."

Joseph let out a hearty laugh, and Stephen could tell that Joseph had relaxed quite a bit around him. The conversation on the merits of reboots of classic films came to a halt and Stephen tried to think of an elegant way to segue into more serious topics.

Somber discussion had always been an issue for him. Joking around was his typical way of communicating, but there were

Guarded Desires

times when dialing it back and being sincere was more appropriate. He'd alienated men in the past by being too much of a jokester. Even if Joseph seemed to enjoy his verbal antics—and had his own dry wit that could match Stephen's—they still needed to be able to have a forthright conversation.

Stephen leaned forward. "Here, I'll grab these."

Joseph reached for the paper plates and empty pizza box. Stephen picked up the beer bottles and followed Joseph into the kitchen. He knew better than to make the same move on the young man as he had before. Or *any* move, for that matter. Not until they'd opened up some more to each other.

As they quietly cleaned up, Stephen pondered what to say next. Joseph regarded him as if he were expecting Stephen might try something. Stephen blurted out the first thing that came to mind.

"Would you like another beer?"

They'd already had three each over the last few hours, but Stephen figured they'd both needed them.

"Actually, I wouldn't mind a soda if you have one."

"Yeah, sure. Cola fine?"

Joseph nodded. "Thanks."

Stephen grabbed two sodas from the fridge, offering one to Joseph. He noted that Joseph was careful to take it from the bottom as if he didn't want to touch Stephen's fingers.

Hmm. Not a great sign.

He couldn't keep from over-analyzing every small thing that happened between them. But Stephen had finally admitted to himself over the course of the evening that he was really falling for the sweet and sexy guardsman.

"Shall we?" Stephen indicated to the living room.

Joseph wouldn't meet his eyes, and there was a tension to his stance that hadn't been there over the course of the evening, his shoulders set and his movements stiff. Still, he went ahead of Stephen and dropped onto the sofa in the same spot as he had before.

Once he was seated as well, Stephen waited for Joseph to begin. He didn't want to pressure him into anything, wanted Joseph to take the lead.

Joseph bit his bottom lip before lifting his gaze to meet Stephen's. "I like you. A lot. You didn't misunderstand me the other night."

Stephen schooled his expression even though he was thrilled at Joseph's words. Joseph clutched the can of pop in both hands as he leaned forward with his elbows on his knees. He lowered his eyes again.

"It's just..." Joseph cleared his throat and muttered, "Fuck." He locked gazes with Stephen and spoke with more intent. "I haven't been in any type of relationship since all the shit that went down with Dorian. I hooked up a couple times, but that's not really my thing. Also, I don't feel comfortable not knowing the guy I'm with. I was young enough when I got with Dorian that I hadn't learned much about what relationships are supposed to be about. Then he..." Joseph's breath seemed to catch in his throat. "All the shit he did to me... It was super fucked up. That's why I get freaked out if I feel someone's going to overpower me."

Rage built in Stephen again over how that animal had treated Joseph. "Is my size a problem?"

He knew there were guys out there that were turned off by bulky, hairy men—he'd certainly met a few. Joseph might like him in general, but if he preferred someone with softer or smoother characteristics, their camaraderie would only carry them so far.

"No. But yes." Joseph cringed. "Dorian was a huge guy, extremely attractive and exactly my type. In the first couple months we were together, other than a few bursts of temper, he

Guarded Desires

was really good to me. I was so taken with him in the beginning, so flattered that he'd want me because he's so damn hot, that I wanted us to spend every waking moment together.

He shook his head. "I was really young and stupid about those kinds of things, and I guess I hero-worshiped him in a way. But then, after we'd been together a bit, I told him I needed to go visit my aunt for the weekend. He fucking went ballistic. That was the first time he beat me, and it was terrible. Bad enough that I knew never to question or assert myself again. Dorian also made it quite clear that I was his property and could never leave. He repeatedly threatened to kill me if I did."

Stephen's stomach turned. He'd give anything to go and pound on that Dorian character, give him a taste of the horror he'd put Joseph through.

"At one point, I decided I didn't care if he killed me or not, I had to get away. He was busy in another part of the house doing one of his deals, and had forgotten to lock the bars over the window like he usually did." Joseph shrugged. "Or maybe he figured I was too chicken to try anything, who knows. Anyway, I escaped and when he found me the threats took on a different edge. This time it wasn't me he would kill, but my family, burn my aunt's ranch to the ground, and her along with it. Make me watch while he..."

Joseph choked on his words and Stephen instinctually moved to comfort him but stopped himself before making contact. Joseph needed to give him consent—is he ever did.

Joseph seemed to gather himself. "Make me watch while he tortured and killed my mom and sister. So, I went back willingly and essentially gave up trying to fight him after that. It no longer mattered whether I did something to provoke him or not, he'd get turned on by hurting me. One of his favorite things to do would be to beat me with his belt, making sure both the leather and the buckle made their mark. Other times he would taunt me with a lit cigarette while I was tied up. Then he would fuck me."

Nausea washed over Stephen, fury gripping him. The need to retaliate on Joseph's behalf was becoming almost too hard to resist, but he knew that nothing positive would come out of him doing so. He also forced himself not to look at Joseph with pity. It wasn't what the man needed.

"I am so incredibly sorry, Joseph. I don't have the words to express my revulsion and hatred at what that fucking bastard did to you."

Joseph chuckled, but with no humor. "Yeah. Me neither."

Stephen sat with his hands clasped in front of him in a similar stance as Joseph. He angled his body in Joseph's direction.

"I will say that I'm very impressed at how you've turned your life around. You didn't allow yourself to fold, become a professional victim, and that's a lot to be proud of. In addition, you've worked hard to become a man the Guard can be proud to have in their ranks."

Joseph ducked his head. "Thanks, but I did it for me more than anything. I didn't want to feel weak anymore, like someone could ever hurt me physically again. That's the reason I've stayed away from relationships. Not because I'm afraid of getting my heart broken, but because the only guys that really do it for me are built like you. And *those* are exactly the types of guys that scare the crap out of me."

Stephen took a moment to absorb Joseph's confession. "I see." Stephen ran a hand over his cropped hair, rubbing the top a few times. "Um, so I guess what you're saying is that I should quit fantasizing about you night and day 'cause it's never gonna happen?"

Stephen attempted a big smile, but knew that it was pretty

feeble. There was really nothing to joke about in their situation. Joseph's expression radiated hurt, and Stephen wasn't sure how to interpret it.

Joseph licked his lips before speaking. "I don't want you to. Stop fantasizing, I mean. Because I've been doing the same."

Joseph set down his drink and scooted closer to Stephen. Holding his breath, Stephen knew he could frighten Joseph off if he made the slightest move toward. Joseph needed to be the one to come to *him*.

Joseph gently placed his hands on Stephen's clasped ones. He stroked them, then reached farther to softly caress Stephen's forearms, moving in even more. He tilted his head back as if in invitation.

"I've never really been kissed, and I want you to be my first."

The fuck?

It seemed like a bad time to interrogate Joseph about what he'd just said, so he filed it away for later.

Stephen lowered his head to capture Joseph's lips and remembered his sweet taste from their first brief encounter. Pushing his way in, he stayed gentle, allowing Joseph time to process the moment. Joseph opened up, answering back with his own tongue. Each swipe, each shared taste increased Stephen's yearning.

As Joseph clutched Stephen's biceps, he pressed his firm body against Stephen and let out a low moan. Stephen ached to take Joseph in his arms but feared it would scare him off again.

Joseph broke the kiss and peered up at Stephen through hooded eyes. "Please hold me. I need you to."

Moving carefully, he pulled Joseph to him, gathering him onto his lap. Joseph placed his arms around Stephen's neck and embraced him as though his life depended on it. It was obvious

Joseph was starved for genuine affection and it broke Stephen's heart.

Joseph buried his face in the crook of Stephen's neck, and Stephen rested his chin on the top of his head. Tentatively at first, then with more intensity, Stephen kneaded and stroked Joseph's back.

With a soft sigh, Joseph adjusted their positions so he was straddling Stephen. Joseph still clutched Stephen's neck, rocking his body against Stephen's hard dick—still encased in the damnable jeans—and placed feathery kisses along the side of Stephen's neck. Joseph returned each squeeze and caress Stephen gave, his touches driving Stephen insane with need.

Joseph angled back and claimed Stephen's lips. This time, Joseph's kiss was greedy and powerful as he used his tongue to delve deeper and deeper, thrusting with growing intensity as he plundered Stephen's willing mouth.

For the first time, Stephen allowed himself to be submissive to his partner. Even though he was on fire for Joseph, possessed with the urge to throw him on the couch and pound into his nice tight ass, it would also be incredible to have Joseph top him.

Their bodies writhed together, Stephen responding to each of Joseph's grinds with his own. If they weren't going to fuck soon, Stephen would simply blow his load in his pants. Joseph broke the kiss, but remained close, their frantic breaths mingling.

"I want us to make love, but I can't... Not tonight."

Stephen caressed Joseph's shoulders, hoping to reassure him. "It's all right, we can stop."

Joseph shook his head. "No. I meant I'm not ready to fuck, to go that far. But if you get rid of your clothes, I'll suck you off."

Stephen's eyebrows shot up as Joseph moved off his lap to

Guarded Desires

give him room. Fumbling with his belt, his body shaking from arousal, he abruptly stopped as Joseph grabbed his wrists.

"Wait. Let me do that."

Joseph pressed his lips together, his brow furrowed into a scowl. Stephen grimaced. He remembered what Joseph had said about what Dorian liked to do before fucking him.

"Whatever you want, it's okay."

Joseph nodded, seemingly unable to meet Stephen's eyes. He unbuckled Stephen's belt then slowly pulled it from the loops. Once he had it free, he tossed it far away from them. Stephen leaned farther back to give him room, Joseph's actions becoming more certain as he unzipped Stephen's jeans and tugged at them. Stephen lifted his butt so Joseph could yank his pants down and off.

Once those were discarded, Joseph paused, and the thought went through Stephen's mind that this might be as much as he could deal with for one night.

Joseph regarded him with a look of determination. "Take off your shirt."

It sounded like a command and Stephen couldn't help but smile. The kid turned him on more than Stephen had expected he would. If things worked out, Stephen thought he might enjoy switching things up a bit.

Stephen yanked off the snug tee then let it drop to the floor. Joseph pushed him back against the throw pillows by his shoulders, then straightened before beginning to remove his own clothing. He never took his eyes off Stephen's body, still clad in a pair of white boxer briefs, the outline of Stephen's full length quite prominent.

Joseph discarded his shoes, socks and belt. He held the bottom of his shirt and it seemed as if he was about to pull it over his head. But he stopped, letting go of the hem. Stephen noticed his breathing had sped up, but it didn't seem to be from arousal.

"Joseph?"

Joseph frowned and shook his head as though he were making up his mind about something.

"I'm okay."

He resumed disrobing, this time taking his shirt all the way off, dragging his white undershirt with it. Stephen immediately saw what the hesitation had been—the scars. Thin lines scattered amongst round burn marks decorated his torso. All Stephen saw was the front, but he imagined the back was as bad, if not worse. There were some smaller stripes on his upper arms, and Joseph self-consciously crossed an arm in front of himself, using his hand to grasp the opposite one.

Stephen felt a renewed rush of admiration for the obvious strength and determination Joseph possessed. And from an aesthetic point of view, the awful marks did nothing to detract from Joseph's masculine beauty. A tight six-pack, hips that narrowed into a V and muscled definition spoke of someone who worked hard to take care of his body—as well as to overcome a brutal past.

"You turn me on so much, Joseph," he said softly. "You're absolutely beautiful and I can't wait to see the rest of you."

Joseph bit his bottom lip and Stephen's thoughts strayed to that gorgeous mouth encasing his swollen cock and sucking it to an explosive conclusion.

"You don't have to say that." Joseph wouldn't meet his eyes.

"I know I don't, but it's the damn truth. I can't make you believe that, but I hope in time you'll get to know me enough to realize I'm an honest and trustworthy man."

Joseph raised his eyebrows. "In time?"

"Yeah." Stephen struggled with how to say the next part. He was still mindful of what would be the best way to proceed

Guarded Desires

with Joseph, yet he also felt it was advisable to get out his true intentions. "I'm not just trying to get into your pants, even though I most definitely *want* to get into your pants." Stephen chuckled, then in a more serious tone he added, "I'd like it if this were to become something more. I hold a lot of respect for you. You're smart, sexy and I think we would get along really well together."

Joseph broke into a big smile and Stephen was glad he'd decided to speak up about his feelings.

"Thank you, Agent Morris. I think we would too." He tilted his head with a slight smirk. "Did I mention how much I love brawny, hairy men?"

Stephen tapped his chin with one finger. "Hmm. Something of that nature does come to mind. Why?"

Joseph's grin grew wider. "Because I'm loving what I'm seeing lying on the couch."

Stephen rubbed the front of his briefs, cupping his balls, anxious to get close to Joseph again. Joseph continued disrobing, and as soon as his dick popped free from his briefs, Stephen couldn't wait for his turn to take him deep into his mouth.

Too much time had passed since he'd inhaled the alluring musk of a man, felt the soft steel of a hot swollen cock on his tongue. Stephen quickly peeled away his own briefs, anxious to get skin to skin with him.

"Jesus. You're incredible, Joseph. I'm going to come just from looking at you." He gestured with his hands for him to move closer. "C'mere babe."

Stephen held out his arms and Joseph moved into them, climbing back onto his lap. Joseph caressed and stroked him some more, Stephen achingly aroused as they ground their hard dicks against each other. Running his fingers through the generous hair on Stephen's chest, arms and torso, Joseph claimed Stephen's mouth, still maintaining the control, Stephen giving in to the demands of Joseph's kiss.

Joseph pulled back and whispered, "I can't believe I never did this before."

Stephen must have had a confused expression because Joseph continued, "Kissing. I love it. But I'm glad you were my first."

A well of emotion rose up in Stephen's throat and he swallowed past it. "I'm honored that I was."

Joseph beamed. After one more quick but searing kiss, Joseph wriggled down the length of his body and captured Stephen's cock into his mouth. Groaning, Stephen arched before thrusting in, grasping the couch cushions at the top and sides to prevent himself from grabbing Joseph. Even in the frenzy of desire, he was mindful not to frighten the young man.

Joseph explored the length of Stephen's cock with his tongue, holding onto the base as he did. There was a sweet suctioning pull each time Joseph moved off his dick, accompanied by a furious licking on the underside of the head. Sometimes, he'd dip into the slit, mercilessly teasing him. It was almost too much sensation, yet Stephen wanted to give in to Joseph completely.

At last, Joseph picked up a rhythm, taking Stephen farther into his mouth each time, opening up his throat to swallow him to the root. As Joseph's pace on his cock increased, the vibrations drove Stephen right to the edge. Joseph had said he wasn't ready for any kind of penetration, but Stephen wasn't sure if Joseph was okay with him coming in his mouth.

Joseph kept his fist tightly wrapped around the base of Stephen's cock, not letting up on the amazing blow job. He doubted he could hold back much longer.

Through erratic breaths, Stephen managed to choke out a quick warning. "Joseph...can't... I'm gonna..."

Guarded Desires

As the first wave of his orgasm slammed into him, Joseph took him all the way in, opening himself up as Stephen shot his cum down his throat, jerking repeatedly. Joseph pulled off, inhaling a big gulp of air, not releasing Stephen's dick as it softened. He laid his head on Stephen's thigh, lightly kissing the sensitive skin where Stephen's hip joined his pelvis.

Releasing the grip he had on the sofa cushions, Stephen then lowered his hands to caress Joseph's head and arms.

He's so loving. So sweet.

A renewed rise of anger swept through him when he thought of the monster who had abused Joseph. He stuffed it down, bringing himself into the present. He only wanted it to be about him and Joseph right then.

"My God, Joseph. That was beyond belief."

A low rumble could be felt against his leg, and he realized it was Joseph chuckling. "I'm glad you liked it."

"Are you kidding? I may never come back to earth." He carded his fingers through Joseph's short hair. "But now I want you in *my* mouth."

Joseph ran his hand up and down Stephen's furry leg. "I'm enjoying this, it's really nice."

"Oh, I am too, believe me. However, I think I might have mentioned something about your cock and my mouth? Please don't make me beg. Although I will if you want me to, soldier."

"I won't make you beg, Agent Morris. At least not this time." Joseph winked as he straightened up. "Do you want me to lie back?"

Stephen gestured with his hands for Joseph to get closer. "Not at all. I want you to be in charge. Fuck my face."

Joseph's eyebrows shot up. "Um, really?"

"Yeah. Use me, baby." Stephen waggled his eyebrows up and down, causing Joseph to laugh again.

"Wow. Another first for me."

Stephen brushed his hands up and down Joseph's sides as he crawled forward to get to Stephen's mouth. Stephen grasped Joseph's ass cheeks to help guide him, adjusting his position to allow Joseph room to straddle him. He gazed up at Joseph's beautiful, hard length, then into his eyes as Joseph hovered over him.

"Stunning, babe. Now fuck me."

The first thrust into Stephen's mouth literally took his breath away. He loved it. It had been too damn long since he'd reveled in a man's flavor, basked in the musky aroma. And Joseph was perfect. There was a slight bitterness to the few drops of pre-cum he'd tasted, and Joseph's personal scent threatened to bring his sated cock back to life. He gave everything he had to sucking Joseph off and the young man whimpered with each swipe of Stephen's tongue around the helmeted head of his long shaft.

Joseph's thrusts became erratic, and Stephen knew he must be getting close. He didn't dare penetrate him, but he reached his fingers in between Joseph's crease and lightly brushed his puckered hole. Joseph started slightly at Stephen's touch, so he brought them down to tease the underside of Joseph's ball sac.

Joseph's nuts hugged his body as he spurted his release and he let out a loud cry. Stephen grabbed Joseph's ass cheeks again to hold him all the way in until the final pulsing emptied the rest of his cum down Stephen's throat.

Joseph tried to pull away, but Stephen would only let him go so far. He wanted to rub his face against Joseph's half-erect cock, revel in the stickiness, breathe him in.

"Mmmm. Wonderful." Stephen let go of Joseph's ass. "Will you lie here with me for a bit?"

The enormous smile on Joseph's face gave him the answer and he sank into Stephen's arms, allowing himself to be cradled. They lay still for a few minutes, stroking one another lightly as they relaxed in the afterglow of their lovemaking.

Stephen spoke in a gentle tone. "Are you okay with what we just did?"

Joseph didn't answer right away, and Stephen's stomach dropped.

"More than okay." Joseph paused and Stephen was sure there was something bothering the young man.

"I hope you know you can tell me anything. I want to be here for you like that."

"Actually, that would be awesome. I could really use someone to talk to. I'm just a little worried."

Stephen stroked Joseph's hair and the side of his face. "What is it, babe?"

"I leave in a week. I could request a permanent transfer, but after what happened and my unpaid leave—well, I don't think..."

Stephen squeezed Joseph tighter, his own fear and worry seeping in. He'd already known there would be logistical issues to their relationship—if that was what they were trying for. But they could figure it out if they stuck together.

"I told you I wanted something more than just a quick lay. I'm not going to let you go that easily, you're worth it. I hope you feel somewhat the same."

Joseph clutched Stephen tighter, and it felt so right. He could tell that Joseph wanted everything to work out between them, too.

"I do, but that's what scares me. I don't see how it can work. And you're the first good thing that's happened to me since I can remember." The last word came out on a small sob.

Stephen squeezed Joseph again, nuzzling his forehead, peppering him with soft kisses.

"We're going to work this out, I promise. How much longer do I have you tonight?"

"I don't have to be back until eight o'clock tomorrow morning."

"Will you come to bed with me? We can shower and put in another film if you'd like. But I really want to hold you in my arms tonight while I sleep."

Joseph lifted his head and gazed into his eyes. "I'd like that a lot. Thank you."

Stephen almost burst out laughing. If anyone deserved thanks, it should go to Joseph. Stephen had despaired of finding anyone he wanted to build a life with and here Joseph was, like a rare gift, offering himself to Stephen.

"No. Thank *you*. Now how about that shower? I'll rub your back if you'll rub mine."

Joseph's laugh eased some of the worry in Stephen's gut. "Whatever you want me to rub, I will."

Stephen winked at Joseph. "Now you have yourself a deal."

Chapter Eight

Kissing. *I never knew.*

After getting in the shower, they hadn't been able to take their hands off each other. What began as simply rinsing off turned into a heavy make-out session, Joseph unable to keep from pushing his tongue into Stephen's mouth, claiming him that way over and over. And Stephen's return kisses were better than anything he'd ever experienced.

As they'd washed each other, it had ultimately led to more kissing and stroking until they'd both climaxed again.

Joseph lay tucked securely in Stephen's embrace in bed, naked. An episode of X-Files was on and Stephen had already warned Joseph that it would likely be their first fight.

"Rigo claims I could drive anyone insane with Mulder and Scully."

"Can I ask you something?"

It was the first thing they'd said to one another since they'd gotten into bed and turned the TV on. Joseph assumed Stephen wanted to know more about the time with Dorian.

"Ask me anything you want."

"When you said I was the first to kiss you... How come? I mean, never?"

Joseph snuggled closer to Stephen. It was odd how unafraid he felt with him now, how he didn't mind talking about uncomfortable subjects.

"The only real sexual contact I had was fooling around with a few guys back in High School. We were all inexperienced and our only goal was to come. There wasn't any pretense of affection, nothing like that. A couple of the guys were just willing to get jacked off or their dicks sucked—not because they were gay—but because they were horny and there were no girls around. Or willing girls, I should say."

Stephen cleared his throat. "I take it that Dorian... Sorry, I shouldn't even bring him up."

"It's okay. We should tell each other stuff like this. It's a fair question." Joseph tried to think of the best way to explain it. "I already wasn't used to that type of thing, so when I got with Dorian, it didn't really register with me at first. But as I fell for him, I had the urge to kiss him once, and he pushed me away. He said he wasn't a girl and if I needed to put my lips on anything, his cock and ass were always available."

Stephen caressed Joseph's head and arms. "True romantic, that one. Thank you for telling me." Stephen lifted Joseph's chin up with his finger. "Then may I have the privilege of kissing you some more?"

Joseph answered by opening himself up to Stephen's mouth. They explored one another, using their lips and tongues freely, the heat building between them.

Stephen's cell phone went off and he tensed.

"Fuck."

Stephen let go of Joseph and he was amazed at how he instantly missed their physical closeness.

Stephen answered his cell. "Agent Morris."

Guarded Desires

Joseph assumed it was work related since it was after midnight. He could see by the intensity of Stephen's expression that it must be serious.

"That doesn't make any sense. Do you think it's a set-up?" There was a pause as whoever it was on the other line answered. "Okay, fine. I'll be right down."

Joseph's heart sank. He'd wanted to sleep in Stephen's arms so badly.

Stephen turned to him, reaching up to caress Joseph's face. "You heard. I'll drop you off on the way."

"What's going on?"

They both got out from under the covers, then went on the hunt for clothes. Joseph had gathered his from the living room earlier, then dumped them in a heap next to his side of the bed before their shower.

My side?

He shook the thought out of his head.

"Apparently, there's a group of dealers ready to roll over on the cartel, but they'll only meet us out in the desert in an hour."

"What?"

"I know. It sounds sketchy, but we'll be careful."

"Like hell you will. I'm going too."

Stephen stopped tugging at his jeans and stared intently at Joseph. "No. You're not. I don't even want to think about the different types of trouble you'd be in for going out there tonight. You're already paying for what happened before, and I'd have a hell of a lot of explaining to do as well."

Joseph bristled. "Are you saying you're ashamed of what we're doing? Of people finding out about me?"

Stephen frowned and finished pulling up his jeans. He approached Joseph and opened his arms as if in invitation. It occurred to Joseph how careful he was being by not grabbing him the way he had before.

And I ran out.

Joseph was still irked but he stepped into Stephen's embrace. He knew he was tense, yet he needed to know where he stood with him. He'd said that they would work it out, but Joseph didn't want to be Stephen's dirty secret.

Stephen nuzzled the side of Joseph's head. "That's the last thing going on in my head. I'll shout it out to the whole town once your situation with the Guard is handled and we've decided how we want to go forward. I don't want anyone else's unwelcome thoughts or opinions to interfere with that. It's for us to decide, alone."

Joseph wrapped his arms around Stephen's large frame, running his hands over the hard muscles bunching under his skin, the soft abundant hair on his back so sexy. He knew Stephen was right, but he was terrified at what might happen to his man out there in the dangerous desert.

He felt protective of Stephen, as if he should be the one guaranteeing his safety—the way he had a little over a week before. He still shuddered when he recalled how close Stephen had come to being another notch in the cartel's belt. Even though he knew that Stephen was greatly skilled at his job, the cartel had become unusually crafty and vicious.

"Okay. I'll stay out of it. But I won't be able to rest until I know you're okay. Please call me the minute you come back?"

Stephen cradled Joseph's face in his hands, stroking his cheeks with his thumbs. "I promise." He descended on Joseph's mouth, kissing him tenderly. Stephen gave him one more strong hug, then let him go.

"I'll call you the very minute I can. I'll be looking forward to hearing your voice."

Stephen winked at him, and Joseph smiled. However, worry still weighed down his heart. He couldn't shake the feeling that something was off about the whole situation.

Guarded Desires

* * *

Of all the times they had to get what might be a solid lead on the cartel case, it was when Joseph was in his arms and wrapped snugly around him. Just the thought threatened to spring his dick back to life. Joseph got him hard in a way he hadn't experienced since he was a young and out of control horn dog. The closeness they'd shared that night was something Stephen had craved for a while—the passionate sex, yes—but also the opportunity to talk to someone about personal things that mattered. And the way Joseph had opened up to him about his difficult past had been encouraging.

Joseph had appeared pretty unhappy when Stephen dropped him off, and he'd had to make him promise again he wouldn't do anything stupid, that he would stay put. Stephen knew the young man would do whatever he could to help him but also counted on his good sense to know when to back down.

Two Guard units had been called out and they would also have air support on standby. Stephen and a sleepy-looking Rigo were battle ready themselves, their Kevlar vests and helmets in place. No chances were being taken on an operation such as this.

Sanchez approached them. He'd been the one to get the call.

"Hey, Hank." Stephen gestured a hello. "From what Boyd told me over the phone, you got the call out here?"

"Yeah. It was kind of weird, if you ask me. The call came in through our main line, the one that goes to the detainee building. It was so unexpected, I didn't even have anything to take notes with."

"One more time. They said what now?"

"They want you and Rigo—they specifically asked for Special Agents Morris and Gonzalez—to go to the same outcrop of rocks where Agent Spender was taken out last week."

"Your words or theirs?"

"Regarding...?"

"Did they literally phrase it 'where Agent Spender was taken out'?"

"I believe so. Like I said, they caught me unprepared. Of course, that was probably their plan."

"No doubt."

An insidious thought crept into Stephen's mind. He'd been so distracted by Joseph earlier it hadn't hit him until right then.

"Rigo, if they know who we are, Carla and the kids..."

"Already on it, buddy. I sent them away before I left the house. No one knows where they are, and no one will. I can't take any chances if there's a mole."

"Good."

Stephen's thoughts drifted to Joseph.

No one knows about us. He'll be okay.

They went over the plan, which amounted to Stephen and Rigo heading out to the previous location in a vehicle equipped with a tracker. Two OH-58 helicopters would be at the ready if things went south, and Humvees would be within a mile radius and surrounding the site.

Stephen let Rigo take the wheel. No one could maneuver a vehicle the way he did, and he'd gotten them out of some pretty hellacious incidents in the past.

Once they left the CBP station and were on the road, Stephen thought it might be safe to really talk. It was no longer feasible for them to share anything except with one another. They couldn't take any chances on who the mole might be.

"What's your take on this?"

"I think it's bullshit. I'm a little surprised that Boyd wants us to go out there at all. It seems too easy, too much like it's just being handed to us. And what group of guys is going to roll over on the Vasquez cartel? Their reach is too extensive. Anyone who's spent more than five minutes with them would know that."

"I agree. They're either trying to take us out or distract us."

Rigo nodded, gripping the steering wheel. "Okay, we got about twenty minutes before we get there. Let's go over some possibilities. If they want to smoke us, wouldn't it make more sense to be stealth about it? This way, it's like they've sent out party invitations."

"No kidding. I agree. So, we think it's a distraction?"

"It's undoubtedly a distraction. The question is, from what?"

Stephen mulled over Rigo's query. A thought chilled him. "The main crossing at Nogales. Where are the helicopters coming from?"

"The Armory."

"And the Guardsmen, our guys?"

Rigo gasped. "*Fuck*. Call it in."

With all eyes on the operation going down fifteen to twenty miles away, no one would be watching Sanchez's station, and the only support there would be a few lone CBP agents. They would get picked off like sitting ducks.

"Sanchez isn't answering."

"Try Boyd."

Stephen practically growled. "He's the asshole who sent us out on this pointless exercise. He'll never listen to our theory."

"Try him anyway."

Stephen brought up Boyd's name under the 'favorites' menu on his phone and hit the send button.

Favorites. That's a laugh.

Stephen growled. "This is perfect. He's not answering either."

Stephen racked his brain trying to figure out the best move, knowing they had mere minutes to make a life or death decision.

Rigo gave Stephen a quick glance before facing forward again. "We go back?"

Stephen nodded. "Fuckin' A. Do it."

Rigo slammed the brakes. The car flipped around at a hundred and eighty angle. He punched the gas pedal, then pushed the car up to almost a hundred miles per hour.

"I fucking love these Dodge Chargers."

"No arguments there."

Stephen alerted local police by calling nine-one-one, requesting that they contact the Guard and to warn any back-up coming in that the Vasquez Cartel was behind whatever was going down.

They were within a half mile of the main Nogales border crossing when a flash of light lit up the sky.

"This does not make me happy."

Rigo grunted. "I'm with you, homey. I'm gonna pull this puppy off the main road and take us behind the west tower."

More light flashed to the east and what sounded like a bomb blast could be heard over the sound of the racing vehicle.

"They're using *explosives?*" Stephen squinted into the distance.

"We could use some air support right about now."

Stephen snorted in agreement with Rigo's massive under-statement. "Dammit! Let's just get in position and do what we can. Head over there." Stephen pointed to a small access road near the tower.

The car had barely come to a stop when Stephen jumped out. Rigo was right behind him, and they took cover behind the tower. Stephen grabbed his binoculars and trained them on the area where they'd seen the most action. He was frustrated that

Guarded Desires

he didn't have the night vision. The whole operation had been thrown together too fast. It hadn't given everyone enough time to think things through.

Likely another ploy on the cartel's part.

Very little could be seen. The searchlights that usually kept the area well-lit had been blown out already. It was impossible to tell who might be in trouble or in need of assistance—or even if any of their guys were still alive. Another flash briefly revealed the chilling sight of men down before everything went dark again.

"I'm moving in closer." Stephen glanced at Rigo who was crouched with him against the tower.

Rigo scrubbed his face with one hand. "Then I'm getting the M4 out of the trunk. I'll cover you."

"You can't even fucking *see* me."

"You have another plan?"

Another loud blast near them hurled a spray of dirt and gravel against the tower.

"*Jesus*. Grenades. It's like a fucking war zone out here." Stephen sucked in a deep breath. "Grab the rifle—but hurry. Who knows when help will get here and we have men down."

Rigo was already racing toward the car. As soon as he threw the trunk open, bullets ricocheted off the Dodge. Stephen could barely see anything as there was only a quarter moon to work with, but there was no movement near the car. Either Rigo had been hit or he'd taken cover.

Stephen gritted his teeth. He couldn't leave his partner. The patrol area would have to wait.

Staying low to the ground, Stephen scurried over to their vehicle and hurled himself down in the dirt behind the trunk. He almost landed right on Rigo.

"Watch it, homey, " he gritted through his teeth. "I took a bullet."

Stephen's heart droppped. "Where?" He couldn't keep the panic out of his voice.

"Left thigh. You won't be insulted if I can't dance with you later?"

"Shut up and let me see."

There was barely enough light for Stephen to tell that if they didn't get help fast, Rigo would bleed out. The grimace on Rigo's face told of his partner's pain, but Stephen couldn't focus on that. He undid his belt and wrapped it around Rigo's thigh above the entry wound. He cinched it tightly and Rigo jerked his leg, remaining silent but no doubt in agony.

"Lie down, buddy. I'm getting help."

"Good luck with that, we've been on our own so far."

Stephen removed his regulation jacket, rolled it up and placed it under Rigo's head.

"Where are the fucking OH-58s?"

They would have infra-red and everything else needed to locate the threat and to direct ground support.

Stephen wrenched his cell phone from his pocket, contacting emergency services again to advise them of the need for several ambulances. He also let them know that he and Rigo were located by the west tower.

The gunfire and grenades had given way to an eerie silence in the past couple of minutes. Stephen was hopeful it was a sign that things had calmed down, that maybe the immediate threat had passed.

The low hum of the Guard helicopters filled the night along with the blare of several sirens as emergency vehicles careened down the main access road. The distinctive noise of the Humvee military trucks rumbled nearby as headlights shone in their direction. Medical help had arrived, and Stephen exhaled for what seemed like the first time since their whole nightmare had begun. Within minutes, triage had been

Guarded Desires

performed on Rigo, and he was loaded into an ambulance. Stephen ached to be able to accompany his partner, but he still had a job to do.

"You owe me a new belt!"

Rigo flipped him off and after the medical van was closed up, it took off wailing down the road.

Stephen waved at one of the Humvees. "You headed up to the main building?"

A Guardsman nodded. "Yeah. Need a lift?"

Stephen squeezed into the back. Now that Rigo had been taken care of, he was anxious to find out what the hell had just happened and if Sanchez was okay.

They arrived at the detainee structure a couple of minutes later and Stephen hopped out of the truck. Mass chaos surrounded him at every turn, with men and women from the various agencies rushing about. Some stood in small groups, seemingly to go over the unbelievable events that had just occurred.

Might as well be in Afghanistan at this point.

Stephen hurried to the place where he hoped he would find Sanchez unharmed. Just as he reached the detainee building, the prospect that Sanchez had escaped unscathed was dashed. He spotted the border agent strapped to a gurney. His eyes were closed, so Stephen directed his inquiry to the medic attending to him.

"How is he?"

"Just some shrapnel, but he took a bump to the head. He's not very coherent, so we're taking him in for observation. He should be fine."

"Okay, thanks."

Stephen whipped his head around, trying to pick Special Agent Boyd out of the confusion. He spied him over by the main crossing gate, conversing with what seemed to be some of the high-ranking Guardsmen. Stephen trotted over, hoping to get an insight on what had gone down before he and Rigo had gotten there. It was obvious Boyd hadn't spotted him yet. He was in deep conversation with the military men.

"They really got the jump on us. If Sanchez and I hadn't been inside the building when it all blew up, we would have been one of the casualties."

Casualties. Shit.

"Boyd, over here."

Boyd's expression radiated shock as their eyes met, and Stephen figured the agent must have assumed that he and Rigo were at the other location meeting with the cartel members.

"Agent Morris, good to see you. I take it you and Agent Gonzalez got some sort of intel about this? I wish you could've given us fair warning."

Stephen frowned. How could they have possibly received any intel on what had happened? They'd barely been gone ten minutes before everything went to hell.

"No intel. Just gut instinct. And we tried to raise both you and Sanchez, but no one picked up their phones."

"We were a little pre-occupied with defending our lives." Boyd seemed to be chewing something over in his mind. "Good instincts, huh? Do we know what's going on at the location where you were *supposed* to be?"

Stephen bit back his anger. "We were a little pre-occupied ourselves. Rigo took a bullet."

"Oh? How is he?"

Jesus. Don't act so concerned.

"He's on his way to the hospital, but I think he should be fine. I'm going over there to check on him as soon as things get wrapped up here."

"Go on ahead. We can have a briefing at the office around eleven."

Guarded Desires

"I don't understand, shouldn't I be here to—"

"What for? From the sounds of it, you didn't meet with the cartel, and you only made it back here in time to get your partner shot. We've got things covered."

Don't slug him, don't slug him, don't slug him.

Stephen clenched his fists but kept them resolutely at his side. Boyd regarded him expectantly, and Stephen forced himself to answer the man who he hoped would soon be his ex-boss.

"Eleven o'clock. Got it."

Chapter Nine

J oseph stared at the ceiling. At least he knew it was the ceiling because he was lying face up on his bed, but he couldn't really see it. The room was very dark, and it seemed as though the night would never end. Stephen was out in the desert facing some unknown danger and all Joseph could do was wait. Wait to hear whether he was okay or not.

The urge to somehow convince him that he should go along or to sneak out had been overwhelming. Yet, he'd also realized that would be foolish. They would both probably put each other in worse danger out of fear for the other's safety, even if he didn't take into account how much trouble he would get in from the Guard.

Helplessness was not Joseph's friend. The two years with Dorian instilled in him a revulsion toward any loss of control.

His mind drifted to the glorious sexual encounter he'd shared with Stephen. The only moment he'd hesitated or thought he couldn't handle them being together was when Stephen had moved his hand to his belt. Never for a second

Guarded Desires

had he believed Stephen would use it on him—it had been more of a knee-jerk reaction.

After that brief hiccup, he'd been okay. Actually, he'd been thrilled.

Stephen had the potential to be all that Joseph had ever hoped for. He still couldn't picture how it would work in the long run, yet Stephen had been so reassuring, so certain about giving them a chance. Joseph couldn't help but get caught up in his enthusiasm.

Joseph glanced at the digital clock. *Four-thirty. Fuck.*

His time off didn't officially end until eight. However, he'd then be required to head to the armory for some target practice and he wouldn't be allowed to have his cell phone on him. He didn't know how he'd make it through the day if he didn't hear from Stephen before it was time to leave.

Trying to sleep was pointless, so Joseph rolled out of bed and onto the floor to do some push-ups. After completing thirty, the exhaustion in his body took over and he thought he might be able to get a little rest. Climbing back in bed, he kept his phone by his pillow so he wouldn't have to fumble for it in the dark.

Right as he dozed off, the ringtone sounded. He startled, then grabbed it, ecstatic to see Stephen's name on the caller ID.

"Thank God." He blurted out.

Stephen chuckled. "I'll say. It was a little dicey out there tonight."

Joseph's blood seemed to freeze, an unpleasant numbness washing over him. "But you're okay, right?"

Stephen sighed. "I'm fine. I'll tell you all about it later. Right now I'm missing you very much."

Joseph smiled despite the lingering worry over what had gone down. "I'm feeling the same."

"We should probably do something to fix that."

"I'm back on duty in a few hours."

"Pesky National Guard. Oh well, I suppose you guys do defend our country, so I'll cut you some slack. When's your next bout of freedom?"

Joseph pondered his schedule. He'd only have one more solid evening of a few hours before he left, then that would be it. "Thursday night from six to midnight. Then Saturday morning, we all pack up and go." Joseph knew he sounded disheartened, but he couldn't help it.

"It's okay, babe, I told you we'd figure it out. Have faith in me."

Joseph smiled. "I do. And you're really okay?"

"I really am. Even better now that I've heard your voice. I can't say plan on Thursday because anything could happen with this case, but plan on Thursday. If there's any way we can get together, I'll make it happen."

Joseph's smile turned to a grin. "Then it's a go on my end."

"Perfect. We can have a six-hour X-Files marathon."

"Make it three and you have a deal."

"My kinda guy. You got it."

* * *

Rigo was going to be laid up for a while and Stephen was more nervous than ever about the situation with the cartel. There was such concern regarding the safety of Carla and the kids, Rigo hadn't dared to contact them from the hospital. Stephen had run out and purchased a burner phone so Rigo could let her know he'd be all right.

Stephen rubbed the back of his neck and yawned. His exhaustion, combined with the crappy chair he was sitting in at his desk, wasn't helping him dissect the case details with much clarity.

Guarded Desires

The eleven o'clock briefing with Boyd and the rest of the team had been less than informative. It was surmised that requesting to meet Stephen and Rigo at the other location had indeed been a way to divert attention from the main border crossing. The question remained, though, as to the primary objective of the bloodbath.

Stephen had his own theories, but until he knew for sure who the mole was—and he was more convinced than ever there was one—he was going to keep his thoughts between him and Rigo. Since his partner couldn't help him out in the field, Stephen would be on his own until the agency assigned a temporary replacement. And because the replacement might be the informer, Stephen would have no choice but to work the case himself.

So, he went back to the beginning to examine all the earliest info he and Rigo had compiled on the Vasquez cartel. The ruthless attack at the main border crossing continued to plague him. If only he could banter with Rigo the way he usually did, he might have an epiphany.

Another important aspect they hadn't fully investigated yet was how the recently deceased Antonio might fit into the picture. Both he and Rigo assumed that Antonio was connected to the cartel, but in what way, they had no idea.

The tediousness of the work began to get to him. He'd spent a large amount of time researching on his computer and using his private phone to make calls. So far, all he'd been able to uncover besides what was listed in Antonio's criminal file was that he was originally from the state of Jalisco, Mexico. His family had a respectable history of making a high-grade agave tequila and were well known in the region.

After some early run-ins with Mexican authorities, Antonio had dropped off the radar for a few years until he'd joined forces with Dorian in the Phoenix area. They'd both been arrested and put away during the DEA sting that had saved Joseph.

He must've lived in terror every single day. Had I only known him then.

Regret never did anyone any good and Stephen focused on the fact that he could be there for Joseph in the present. His current situation with Joseph, the overwhelming case load and his own crippling exhaustion finally forced him to fold up the files and lock them back in his desk for another day.

It seemed as if he wouldn't be going out in the field any time soon and he wasn't sure how he felt about that. On the one hand, he understood the need to protect him and Rigo now that they were known to the cartel. On the other hand, the frustration he felt at being hobbled was very difficult. There was the consolation of getting together with Joseph on Thursday, but he'd had some recent concerns about that, too.

What if he becomes a target because of me?

"Shit."

An agent passing his desk stopped. "Everything okay?"

Stephen glanced up at Agent Nelson, a guy he'd trained with back at Quantico and who'd shown up after being assigned to the Tucson sector six months ago. He, Nelson and Rigo had gone out a few times to shoot some pool and knock back a few beers. He considered him a close acquaintance, if not a friend.

But could he be a rat in their nest?

"Nah, just long hours with everything going on recently. But it's getting late, so I should head on home."

"You still have police protection at your place, right?"

"Oh yeah. Don't want to take any chances."

"Good." He nodded sagely. "How's Rigo doing?"

"Fine, just fine."

"Is he out of the hospital yet?"

Guarded Desires

Stephen's throat went dry. He didn't care for how Nelson was asking so many questions. Likely, it was innocent. On the other hand, how well did he really know the guy?

"No. They may keep him there for a while longer."

"Good, he should probably take it easy. How are Carla and the kids taking it?"

Stephen cleared his throat but kept his tone casual. "Not great, as you can imagine, but they're hanging in. Listen, I gotta go." Stephen rose from his desk. "I'll tell Rigo you asked about him, I'm sure that'll mean a lot."

"Of course, what are buddies for, right?" Nelson gave Stephen a light fist punch on the side of his arm. "Let me know if I can help with anything."

"Yeah, sure." He gave him a tight smile. "Thanks."

Stephen hurried from the office, hoping he didn't look too anxious to leave.

Next stop: get another burner phone.

* * *

A few days had passed since he last spoke with Stephen, and it was starting to seem as if Joseph had overestimated how interested Stephen was in pursuing a relationship. Maybe Stephen was so busy with his job that he'd reconsidered the idea of them being together when there were so many obstacles. Location. Job restrictions. Emotional baggage. Stephen was a total hottie who had a lot to offer. Why would he want to put up with Joseph's crap?

After finishing his duty for the day, he'd resigned himself to kicking back in his room. Lounging in any of the common areas only invited harassment from Barnett and Griffin. The two goofballs were back to being buddies again and were on the prowl looking for trouble. He had a couple of books he'd been wanting to dive into and it would be a good way to occupy his mind and keep it off Stephen.

Right as he woke up his e-reader, his phone went off. His heart jumped in anticipation of it being the sexy agent. A glance at the caller ID had him frowning, though. He didn't recognize the number.

"Hello?"

"Joseph, I'm so glad you picked up."

Happiness swept through him, yet there was an edge to Stephen's tone that worried him.

"Stephen, I'm glad I did too. What happened to your phone?"

"I'm concerned it might be compromised."

Joseph's stomach tightened. "Has something else gone down?"

"Not yet, and I intend to keep it that way." Stephen sighed. "It breaks my heart to consider this, but I'm not sure we should see each other Thursday."

Joseph swallowed past a lump in his throat. He'd stopped trying to pretend the hadn't already fallen hard for Stephen.

"I see." He knew the hurt in his voice was evident, yet he couldn't control it.

"Joseph, please, don't take this the wrong way. It would only be if you don't feel—"

"That's okay, I understand."

"Knock it off, kid. We're going to work this out."

"Seriously, you don't have to—"

"I said knock it off. I'm trying to tell you I have an idea for Thursday, unless you don't feel comfortable seeing me."

Stephen paused, and Joseph thought maybe he'd hung up in anger. He was about to check his phone when Stephen spoke up again.

"How about this. I'm going to call you back on my regular

Guarded Desires

phone and say the same thing to you, but you're going to get so angry that you tell me to go fuck myself. Rigo says it to me all the time, so I'm used to it. Then hang up on me."

Joseph frowned. "Okaaay..."

"If anyone is listening in, they'll think we're not seeing each other Thursday, and if we're *really* lucky, not seeing each other anymore. I'll even add to it tomorrow at work by moping around. There's one agent in particular who's been nosing around my business."

A flicker of hope ignited in Joseph.

"Things are really that bad?"

"I'm just being extra cautious. I can't take a chance on losing you."

Whoa.

"I... Sure. Whatever you think, Stephen."

"Great. I feel better now. I wasn't sure how I was going to last without seeing you before you left."

Joseph winced. They still had that to deal with.

"Before I hang up, we need to figure out how we can meet. Is there anyone there you have a good relationship with, someone you could trust?"

Harrison.

"Actually, yeah. What are you thinking?"

"When it's time for you to get your break Thursday, have him leave with you, like you guys are going to go hang out together."

"That might work. Except I don't know if he has Thursday off."

"Hmm. See if he does because it would look better, otherwise, come and meet me anyway at El Gringo Loco. From there, we can go to a motel somewhere for a few hours."

"Are you taking me to a seedy motel, Agent Morris?"

"Of course. Doesn't every hot young guardsman want to be

123

wooed at an incredibly low-class dive? I promise you, I'll only treat you to the worst."

"Good to know, since that has always been my fondest dream. What if you're followed to the bar?"

Stephen chuckled. "Are you sure you wouldn't like to pursue a career with the DEA? Actually, I'm going to leave my car at home, sneak out and borrow Carla's. They keep it in the garage and Rigo and I have keys to each other's places."

"Do you think he'll mind?"

Stephen chuckled. "It was his idea. We cooked up this plan together."

Joseph was taken aback. "So...you told him?"

"Of course I did, he's my best friend. Is that okay?"

Joseph couldn't hold back a big grin. "Totally."

"It's a date then?"

"It's most definitely a date."

"You're making me a happy man, Joseph. Now get off the phone so you can break up with me when I call you back."

Joseph laughed. "I'll be looking forward to it."

"Troublemaker."

"You know it."

It seemed as if things might work out after all.

* * *

It worked out perfectly that Harrison could go out with him. The plan was to leave right at six and take a taxi to the bar. Joseph had been hesitant to involve Harrison, but when he explained the situation, his new friend had been eager to help. A couple of the guys from his unit were injured in the operation that had cost Spender his life. He was also happy that Joseph had found someone.

Guarded Desires

"Does your boyfriend know of any other handsome DEA agents looking for a good time?"

Joseph chuckled as he made his way to the housing unit where Private Harrison stayed. He really liked the guy and was hopeful they could remain friends, even if Joseph wouldn't be around the Mesa Armory for a while. Joseph cringed a little—that would need to be discussed when they got together.

Harrison was already waiting outside, ready to go. They greeted each other casually, waiting until they got on the main road before getting into any real conversation. After walking for a few blocks, they reached a convenience store where Joseph called for a cab.

"Thanks again, Dan. I really appreciate it."

"No problem. I've been bored out of my mind anyway."

"Have any of the guys in your unit seen any more action since last week?"

"Nah. We've been doing the day patrol support the way you've been ever since...well, what happened with you."

Joseph shrugged. "Yeah. I heard it was the Nogales Armory guys stationed here that saw all the action the other night. None of us were even called out."

"That pissed me off. Drag us all the way out here and I slept through the entire thing."

"I guess they have their reasons."

The taxi pulled up and Joseph's heart raced at the thought of seeing Stephen in a few minutes. He wasn't supposed to acknowledge him. He and Harrison would grab a couple of beers and sit down. Stephen would already be there to make sure he hadn't been followed. When he was sure it was clear, he would head to the men's room, but actually go out of the back door where he had Carla's car parked. Joseph would follow a minute later and do the same thing.

The cab driver dropped them off in front of El Gringo Loco

and Joseph focused on maintaining his composure. He couldn't even lock eyes with Stephen—it would be too obvious if anyone was watching them.

As they pushed into the dark establishment after coming in from the bright sun, Joseph rubbed his eyes, adjusting to the dim surroundings. Joseph caught Stephen to the far left of the room in his peripheral vision and ducked his head.

Don't turn your head, go straight for the bar.

Walking on shaky legs, Joseph tried to act like getting a beer was the most important thing in the world to him.

Harrison was blathering on about something and Joseph was thankful that his friend had taken the initiative to make it seem as though they were merely there to hang out as buddies. All Joseph could think about was being alone with Stephen. They climbed onto the barstools, and Joseph angled his body so he could see the hallway leading to the restrooms.

Beads of sweat broke out on his forehead, his heart thumping so loud he sure the entire bar could hear.

Be patient.

He noticed the movement of someone go past him and took a long pull on his beer. As he did so, he saw it was Stephen headed to the men's room. Lowering his beer, then setting it on the bar, he exchanged some more idle chit-chat, took another quick swig, then got up from the stool. Harrison was supposed to stay there for another ten minutes before leaving.

His nerves on edge, his breathing rapid, Joseph never broke his stride as he hurried to the back door. At that point, the aspects of danger were outweighed by his need to be alone with Stephen. To touch him. To taste him.

Stephen had told him that Carla had a silver Honda, and that he'd already have it running. Only the Honda and an old GMC pick-up were out back, so he didn't have to search too

Guarded Desires

hard. Without even slowing his pace, Joseph yanked the passenger door open and jumped in.

"Crouch down and stay hidden."

"Nice to see you too." But Joseph did as Stephen commanded.

From where he had himself crammed on the floor of the vehicle, Joseph spotted the curl at the edges of Stephen's mouth. After a couple minutes of driving while keeping one hand on the wheel, Stephen reached down to Joseph and helped him back onto the seat.

Joseph buckled himself in, thrilled that Stephen had never let go as he did. As he settled in, he entwined his fingers with Stephen's, the agent stroking the inside of Joseph's wrist as he drove.

"God, you feel good. I hope you don't mind, but I really wanted to take you to the absolute filthiest place that I know of and it's out in the boonies. It'll take us about fifteen minutes to get there."

"The filthier, the better."

Stephen snorted. "Then you'll *adore* this place."

Chapter Ten

"You brought a sleeping bag with you?"

Joseph tried to keep from laughing as Stephen dragged the red not-so-neatly rolled bag from the back of the CRV.

"What part of 'filthy' did you not understand?"

Joseph grabbed the cooler Stephen had also packed, along with a small tote he'd asked him to bring inside.

"You're making some pretty brash assumptions, Agent Morris. Did you think I would be getting into that sleeping bag with you?"

"Hey. You're the one who followed a man out the back door of a dive bar and climbed into his car. I look pretty innocent after all that."

Stephen struggled with the key while balancing the unruly bed roll and finally managed to turn the knob, kicking the flimsy door open. They stepped into the dank room and set everything down. Stephen gingerly placed the red bag on the table. He shut the door and switched on the light, which barely cast a glow.

Guarded Desires

"Ah, I see the room has been done in my favorite décor, Early American Disaster."

Joseph had to agree, the place was rather horrific. A shredded orange and yellow floral bedspread that screamed 'reject from the seventies' said it all. When he added in the cigarette smoke-caked tacky prints and the peeling wallpaper with tomahawks and tepees on it, Joseph was sure he'd never seen anything worse.

But they were most definitely out in the middle of nowhere. And the clerk who had rented them the room for twenty bucks had seemed unlikely to remember his own name, let alone anything about him or Stephen.

"Is this carpet making crunching noises?" Joseph lifted his feet up and down several times.

"Don't take your shoes off. Jesus." Stephen wrinkled his nose. "Maybe we should go back out to the car. Oh, and just in case you were wondering—yes—I'm all about the romance."

Joseph snorted laughter. "I don't care. We're here together." Heat crawled up his neck and into his cheeks.

Stephen regarded him with what could best be described as a wistful expression. "Then let's make this dump our little corner of paradise for the next few hours."

They carefully arranged the sleeping bag to cover the entire bed and after investigating the rest of the room, found what looked to be clean—albeit ragged—bath towels. They placed those on the floor next to bed so they could indeed take off their shoes.

As they silently prepared everything, even dragging the cooler within reach of where they would be lying, a twinge of insecurity shot through him.

He hasn't even tried to kiss or hug me.

Even as the thought entered his mind. he remembered how

129

careful the Stephen had been with him so far. But he had to know it was okay to make a move now, didn't he?

Maybe not.

"I...I liked it when you held me." Joseph shifted from foot to foot. "Before, I mean. The other night."

Stephen straightened from where he'd been placing a couple of cans of soda on the nightstand. He furrowed his brow, and Joseph couldn't tell what he might be thinking. As he took tentative steps forward, it seemed as if he were testing what Joseph's reaction might be.

Joseph scraped his teeth along his bottom lip. "It's okay. I'm not scared of you. I *want* you to want me. To touch me. I might just get nervous once in a while, that's all. But it's honestly okay."

Stephen edged closer to him, seemingly with more assurance. Moving slowly, he gathered Joseph into his arms, the embrace careful, yet sweet. Someday, Joseph hoped they could both completely let go and not allow his past abuse to interfere with their intimacy.

Joseph melted into Stephen's arms and inhaled the slightly spicy cologne mixed with his naturally masculine scent. The smell was like an aphrodisiac to Joseph. He wanted to give Stephen everything, to finally make love, but didn't know if it would be the right time yet, if he could handle it without freaking out.

So far, Stephen had been incredibly patient and loving with him. There wasn't any indicator from the one night they'd spent together that Stephen would pressure him into anything. God, he'd even been willing to stop when things became heated, and Joseph knew that must've taken a lot of willpower.

But someday, Stephen would want to top him. Joseph was sure of it.

"Do you want to talk about anything?"

Guarded Desires

The deep rumble of Stephen's voice tickled his ear that was pressed against Stephen's chest.

"Um, kinda."

Stephen stepped back and took Joseph's hand, and he allowed Stephen to lead him to the bed. Stephen sat down, tugging gently on Joseph as if encouraging him to sit down.

"What is it, babe? Remember, anything you want to say is cool."

Joseph nodded. "That means a lot, actually."

He glanced around as if something in the decay of the room would help him find the words that wouldn't make him sound too pathetic or weird. Stephen held his hand between both of his very large ones, and it felt safe. Comforting. Stephen stroked and caressed them, Joseph closing his eyes to concentrate on the sensation. It was so different, so kind.

His eyes flew open. So would everything else that Stephen did with him. Even if he couldn't go all the way now, he was sure he could one day.

"Are you a top?"

Stephen froze, his movements coming to a halt. "Usually. But it depends on how drunk I am. At that point I can be talked into a lot of things."

Joseph arched his eyebrows.

Stephen winced. "Sorry. Inappropriate?"

Joseph shook his head. "No. Not if it's the truth."

Stephen scrunched up his nose. "If we're doing true confessions, then yeah. In the past that's how it's been."

"How far in the past?"

Stephen raised Joseph's hand to his lips then kissed the knuckles. Then he brought their still-joined hands back down, rested them on his knee.

"At the risk of sounding like a man-whore, it was up until

the last relationship I was in, which essentially ended two years ago when I moved here."

"Essentially?"

"Well, I thought we were going to continue having a relationship and he didn't. Communication is a bitch."

Joseph chuckled. "How long were you guys together?"

"A little over a year."

"And you moved here but he didn't come with you?"

"I wanted him to. And I was willing to keep the relationship going long distance, but he wasn't."

"Really?" Joseph considered that. It added an interesting spin to things. "Do you mind me asking all these questions?"

"It's reassuring. I was afraid you were only using me for my hot body."

Joseph snorted. "How old are you?"

Stephen sighed dramatically. "Ancient is the first thing that comes to mind, but seriously, I'm thirty-six."

Joseph had figured he was mid-thirties, so it was hardly a surprise. "I'm twenty-two. Does that bother you?"

"Hell yes, it does. I only date men who are collecting their Social Security benefits. That way, there's always an income to fall back on. I just assumed you had a really amazing plastic surgeon."

Joseph laughed a little harder. "So, it really doesn't bother you?"

"I'd be an idiot to let your age bother me. You have an intelligence and maturity about you that I find very attractive. And it's not something I've been able to find most of the time, even in men much older." Stephen's light-heartedness returned. "Me, for instance. I'm an excellent example of rampant immaturity. Ask Rigo, he'd be more than happy to vouch for me. He'd probably even be willing to state that I'm not the brightest thing he's ever met either."

Guarded Desires

Still laughing, Joseph tried to bring the topic back to his original question. "Um, but you *do* prefer to top?"

Stephen massaged and caressed the hand that he still held. "Are you worried about that?"

Joseph shrugged, afraid that Stephen might not want to take things any further. "Kinda. Although, I've always bottomed. It was what I always liked until...well, until I didn't. I know it'd be different with you, even better than before. I'd like to try it again, but maybe not yet?"

"Do you want me to bottom for you?"

That made Joseph pause. "I'm not sure. I've never done it before. I don't want you to do it if it's just for me."

Stephen pulled Joseph closer. He let go of Joseph's hands and stroked his arms up and down, keeping his touch light.

"I would love to feel you inside me."

Joseph's face heated again. He rarely did that. Stephen had brought something out in him that was different from what he'd ever experienced with anyone else—a good different.

"Okay." He wasn't sure how to say the next part, but he didn't want his new lover to feel like he had to treat Joseph as if he were a fragile piece of china. "You don't have to be so careful with me. I won't break."

"I felt bad after that first night. I shouldn't have been so insensitive, so pushy."

"It's okay. Even if I react badly to something, I don't want that to keep you from trying. I need to feel your passion for me. It'll just take time for me to tell the difference between desire and anger." Joseph locked eyes with him. "I want to learn that with you."

Stephen pulled Joseph onto his lap with a bit more force. Cupping Joseph's face, Stephen brought their lips together and thrust his tongue into Joseph's mouth, his kiss strong and commanding. Joseph loved the feel of Stephen's beard against his lips. The exchange overtook his senses and he believed that someday, he'd want Stephen to take him in every way he could.

Joseph relaxed against Stephen's muscular body, giving up control. Stephen clutched him tighter, Joseph's cock filling with each swipe of Stephen's talented tongue. Using his large hands to cup Joseph's ass, Stephen gave them a hearty squeeze. His dick was so hard and he ached for Stephen to touch his hole again, to touch him everywhere.

Joseph reluctantly broke the kiss to stare into Stephen's eyes. They were almost nose to nose and Joseph still held the back of Stephen's head so that he couldn't move away.

"Put your fingers inside me. If you want to, I mean."

"Babe...." Stephen dropped a kiss on the end of Joseph's nose. "I want to do that more than you know."

Joseph's breathing picked up a rapid pace. God, the man turned him on so much. He nodded. "I think if we start with that for now, I can work up to more later."

"Can I also taste you there?"

Joseph's breath caught in his throat. "Yeah. I'd like that a lot."

Stephen smiled at and pulled Joseph's head back by his hair, still keeping his touch gentle. "Me too. I hope you don't think it too presumptuous of me, but I did bring some lube in case we needed it."

"I don't think it's presumptuous. Thoughtful would be more like it."

"If you want me to bottom for you tonight, I have condoms as well. But I'll leave that up to you."

Joseph flushed—this time from excitement. He leaked in anticipation, needing them to both get their clothes off immediately. Joseph disentangled himself from Stephen and stood up to hurriedly remove his jeans and shirt. Stephen's face split into a grin, and he reached for his belt. He froze before touching it.

Guarded Desires

"I wasn't thinking, Joseph. I'm sorry."

I can do this. It'll be okay, he won't hurt me.

Even as his hard-on flagged, he willed himself to go through with it, to let Stephen take off the belt. To trust him.

"It's okay. Go ahead."

Stephen drew his eyebrows together. "It doesn't matter. Why don't you—?"

"No. I want you to. I trust you."

The distressed expression on Stephen's face was almost too much to bear, so he tore his eyes away and stared at the belt instead. Stephen moved slowly, obviously mindful of how terrifying the moment must be for Joseph. This man was someone who Joseph could treasure, and he was sure would treasure him in return. He focused on that thought alone, driving the meaning of the belt from his mind.

Once the accessory had been unbuckled and Stephen carefully removed it from the loops of his pants, Joseph was unable to slow his breathing, his hands becoming clammy, the urge to run almost unstoppable. The belt came loose, and as the end hit the edge of the bed, Joseph flinched.

"Oh God, babe."

Stephen tossed the belt behind him, far out of reach from them both. Joseph realized his hands were clenching and unclenching and his breathing had become shallow.

"Talk to me, Joseph. What do you need me to do?"

I must be such an aggravation to him.

Yet Stephen didn't act that way. All he'd done so far was treat Joseph with the utmost care. Then it occurred to him. The belt was nowhere near them. Stephen had removed what had once been a weapon for Dorian and hadn't used it on Joseph. Logically, he'd known that all along—that Stephen would *never* use it on him. But emotionally, as soon as his Stephen had touched it, all reason had left him.

His breathing slowed and he calmed down. Stephen held open his arms, the same as he had before when he allowed Joseph to be in control. Joseph was barely able to move his legs, they seemed so leaden. But he yearned to be cradled in the strength of Stephen's arms. Once he was able to make his cement-filled limbs move, he practically collapsed in the agent's embrace.

Only Joseph's briefs remained and Stephen's soothing caresses on his back were comforting. He closed his eyes and rested his cheek against Stephen's broad shoulder. Joseph lifted his head and claimed Stephen's lips, forcing his way into his mouth and using his tongue to assert control over the kiss, grabbing the back of Stephen's neck as he did.

Joseph loved the way Stephen gave into him. It provided him with the strength he needed to let go. This time, Stephen broke the kiss.

"I want to feel your skin on mine."

Joseph nodded and moved from Stephen's lap. He pulled off his briefs as he watched his sexy man remove his clothing. He was reminded of that first night when the guys went to the strip club and how he'd thought about Agent Morris undressing for him.

Who knew?

He couldn't stifle a giggle. Stephen turned around, a mock look of hurt on his face.

"I should probably head back to the gym if my naked body makes you laugh." His tone was teasing.

Joseph shook his head. "You're awesome, don't worry. I was just thinking about you and strip clubs."

"I only did it that one night, and it was just to work off my bar tab. I swear I never went back. They promised all the pictures had been destroyed."

Guarded Desires

"Except for the ones I bought." Joseph laughed freely, all the tension he'd held in his body releasing.

Still smiling, Stephen approached the bed, his cock half-erect and level with Joseph's mouth.

"Tell me what to do, Joseph." Stephen gazed down at him with affection. "Should I lie down with you straddling my face?"

"I want to suck you a little first. But then, okay."

It didn't seem as if it would be very long before he'd be comfortable enough to allow Stephen to be on top. For now, though, this worked better for him.

Joseph grasped Stephen's thick cock, licking his lips at the sight of pre-cum at Stephen's slit. He stuck out his tongue and lapped up the beads of sticky dew, Stephen's dick twitching as he did. He let the drops melt in his mouth, allowing himself to experience Stephen's flavor.

The last time with Stephen been so heady and thrilling—like gobbling down a dessert but never stopping to appreciate it. They might not have the chance to be together again for a while, and he wanted to memorize everything he possibly could about Stephen.

Before Joseph wrapped his lips around Stephen's heavy cock, he peered up at him.

"You can grab my hair, but let me be the one to move, okay?"

Stephen smiled down at him. "Of course, babe."

Joseph reached around to grasp Stephen's muscular ass cheeks, enjoying the sensation of Stephen running his fingers through his hair and stroking his scalp. Joseph bobbed his head on Stephen's steeled length, taking him in deeper each time. He suckled him but didn't want Stephen to come too soon.

After letting Stephen's dick fall from his lips, he pulled

himself up, still clutching Stephen's wonderful ass. Joseph pressed his body against the hard muscles of Stephen's frame, his cock sliding alongside his man's erection. They held each other's hands, their fingers laced together, their bodies gently swaying.

"Let me make you feel good."

Stephen kept hold of Joseph, stepping back against the edge of the bed and descending down on the mattress. He lay on the red sleeping bag, gently tugging Joseph on top of him. Once Stephen was prone, he let go of Joseph and ran his hands along the backs of Joseph's thighs.

"Straddle me like you did the other night, but stay up on your knees."

Stephen's gentle tone increased his desire. He ached to grab his own cock but wanted to find out what Stephen was going to do first. Stephen twisted his body to retrieve something from the tote bag beside the bed. He pulled a small bottle of lube out and set it next to him.

"I get to taste you, too."

Stephen reached up for Joseph's cock and lowered it to his mouth, capturing the early seed leaking from him.

"Mmm... Very nice. Get up on your knees and move forward. That's it. Now sit on my face."

Joseph hesitated. This was all new to him. Stephen encouraged him by spreading his ass cheeks wide and lifting his head to probe Joseph's entrance with the tip of his tongue. Joseph relaxed, enjoying the erotic feel of the hot, wet tongue.

Stephen licked and explored, laving the inside of his crease until Joseph moved his hips forward and back in a slow, rocking motion. His slit dripped more pre-cum as Stephen lapped at him harder and Joseph clenched around Stephen's probing tongue.

Stephen placed his hands on the tops of Joseph's thighs and urged him farther down farther, kissing and teasing his hole

Guarded Desires

with lips and tongue. He reached around to push Joseph up on his knees, rubbing his hands along the backs of Joseph's thighs.

Then, Stephen mouthed his sac, sucking each heavy ball in turn before reaching for the small bottle of lube. He released Joseph to pour the slick on his fingers and Joseph concentrated on remaining relaxed. Even though he trusted Stephen, and ached for all his touches, being breached was another thing.

"You can tell me to stop at any time. I won't be offended."

Joseph nodded, bracing himself. Stephen continued the teasing touches, playing in Joseph's crease until the urge to press against Stephen's thick fingers overtook him. A slight pressure against his opening caused him to still, but he didn't clench up. More force was applied until one of Stephen's fingers popped into his ass.

While he felt a slight burn, it wasn't painful, and he didn't feel violated. The slickness allowed Stephen to finger fuck him with ease, and Joseph let out a slow breath, giving himself over to the sensation. Stephen used the one digit on him for a minute or so then another finger was pressed against his opening. Stephen gently slid it inside his ass alongside the other.

Joseph couldn't stop himself from clenching around Stephen's fingers. There still wasn't any pain—which surprised him based on his experience with Dorian—but this time, the stretching of his passage was more pronounced. His mind went sideways the moment Stephen brushed against something inside him that sent a tingling sensation right to the tip of his cock and to the base of his spine.

Holy shit. Must be my prostate.

He'd thought he'd felt that before, but it had been brief and encased by so much pain, he hadn't been sure. Done with care, the sensation was quite different. It even gave Joseph more reassurance that he would like Stephen to claim his ass someday. If he was prepared like this, he could imagine it would feel incredible to be fucked hard by him.

Instead, he would do it to Stephen now.

"Let me fuck you, Stephen, please."

Stephen slid his fingers from Joseph's ass. "Do you want to get me ready, or should I do it?"

"I'll do it. Exactly like you just did?"

"If you're going to enter me it would be better if you could put three or four lubed fingers in and stretch me by spreading your fingers apart and twisting your hand." He gave him a lopsided smirk. "It's been a minute."

Joseph nodded, picking up the small bottle then pouring a generous amount onto his fingers. Stephen lifted his knees and held his legs up as if in invitation. Joseph's mouth went dry at the sight of Stephen's puckered hole, his cock throbbing in anticipation of being buried inside him. Joseph squeezed more slick directly on Stephen's wrinkled entrance and he jerked with a gasp.

"Sorry. I forgot that it might be kind of cold."

Stephen gave him a reassuring smile. "That's all right. I want you in me."

Joseph returned his attention to preparing Stephen's hole. Based on his own horrible experiences of being penetrated, the last thing he wanted to do was hurt Stephen. He worked his first finger in, mimicking how Stephen had slid in and out. He added the second one and included a twisting motion. A third and fourth one were introduced, and it was such a turn on to watch as Stephen impaled himself on Joseph's hand, how he writhed and moaned, his cock firming and leaking beads of pre-cum against his belly.

Stephen's reaction filled Joseph with a sense of power, of being able to grant so much pleasure to another human being. "Are you ready for me?"

Guarded Desires

"God yes, Joseph. I can't remember ever saying this to anyone before, but I really want you to fuck me. Hard."

Stephen's words alone threatened to make Joseph come, so he hastily ripped open the condom. As he covered his dick with it, he was so sensitive that rolling the rubber over his tip almost set off his release.

Joseph paused, steadied his breathing, and gave himself a chance to gain some control. He poured a more of the cool slickness on his heated length and that helped to stave off his orgasm. Grabbing himself at his root, he poised his cock at Stephen's twitching entrance. As he nudged against Stephen's tight hole, worry overtook him. The fear of hurting Stephen threatened to kill his erection.

Stephen grabbed Joseph's wrist. "You'll have to push into me with a little force. I promise you won't hurt me."

Joseph nodded and bore down at the same instant that Stephen thrust up. He breached Stephen's opening and sank into his channel, his stiff flesh encased by soft heat. With a groan, he moved inside Stephen, driving deeper and deeper. Joseph leaned down, licking at Stephen's nipples set in his hairy chest, bringing them to attention.

As the speed of Joseph's fucking increased, Stephen's hard cock bobbed against Stephen's belly. Joseph grasped the base, sliding his fist along the rigid shaft, stroking him in time with his thrusts.

Their combined moans added to the sounds of their bodies slapping together, a fine sheen of sweat building between them. Joseph gripped Stephen's thigh to give him more leverage as he jerked him off, slamming his cock into Stephen's ass with a need he'd never experienced.

"Yeah Joseph, come with me, babe, come..."

Warmth spilled over his hand right as Stephen's snug passage fluttered around his cock. With a yell, Joseph shot his load into the condom, gritting his teeth as he rode the first waves of his climax.

The pulsing continued a few seconds longer as the last bit of cum was squeezed from his spent cock. Sweat poured down his face and body, his frantic breathing gradually slowing. Joseph wanted nothing more than to collapse on top of Stephen, but he took care to grab the condom at the top as he softened and slipped out of him.

As he leaned over to drop the condom onto one of the towels, Stephen wrapped his arms around Joseph and gathered him to his chest. Now that Stephen had stretched out his legs, and Joseph was draped across the length of his body.

He marveled at Stephen's solid, muscular form, and that he no longer found it threatening. Stephen had given himself to him, had let him have all the control, let him be the one to penetrate him. And he he'd shown him just how good it could be.

They only had a couple of more hours together, then it would be time to head back. His chest tightened as he fought back tears. He'd give anything to stay even one night in Stephen's arms. To know what it would be like to wake up with him.

Joseph tried not to think about the challenges they would face as a couple. After what they'd just shared, along with how comfortable he'd been discussing difficult subjects with Stephen, Joseph had to believe they would find a way to make it work.

He couldn't imagine facing life without his loving bear by his side.

Chapter Eleven

The car was packed, and Stephen noted there was about another fifteen minutes left before they had to leave. They'd both become quiet, and Stephen knew it was the knowledge that this was the last time they'd see each other for the foreseeable future.

The moment weighed heavily on them.

Stephen opened his arms. "I want to hold you on my lap, babe. We have a few more minutes and I'd like to make plans. Give this my full attention before we get in the car."

Joseph appeared puzzled, his brow furrowed as he chewed his bottom lip. Stephen knew the young man tended toward cynicism. Not that he blamed him after all he'd been through in his short life. After another beat, Joseph fell into his embrace.

Joseph rested his head in the crook of Stephen's neck. "How can we make plans? You don't know yet what's going to happen with the case."

"You have unpaid leave, right?"

"Well, yeah. But I'll be back in Phoenix at my mom's."

"Do you want to stay with your mom for the sixty days?"

"Not necessarily. I just don't have anywhere else I can go."

Stephen cleared his throat. "You can stay with me."

Silence fell between them, and Stephen thought he might've gone too far.

"What about the whole cartel threat?"

Stephen groaned. "I'll find somewhere safe you can stay. I'll visit you."

Joseph clung to him tighter. "That's not going to work, and you know it. As much as I want to be with you, I can't hide out somewhere by myself waiting for stolen moments when we can be together. And I don't want to be living off you either. At my mom's I can always get my old job back at the hardware store. We've known the owner for years."

Stephen let out a sigh. "And you'd be safer there. But God, Joseph. I don't know if I can stand to be away from you for very long."

Joseph clutched Stephen's shoulders and he raised his head. "I'm not sure I can either." Joseph locked eyes with him. " Will you wait for me? Until things calm down? I understand if you don't want to, but I wish you would."

Stephen pressed his lips to Joseph's, forcing his way in to sweep his mouth with his tongue, conveying all his need to the man who'd stolen his heat. He broke the kiss and grabbed the back of Joseph's head.

"I'll wait for you, Joseph. If things don't get wrapped up with the cartel right away, we can still meet somewhere between here and Phoenix. I'll do whatever it takes to be with you, even if it can only be once in a while."

Stephen surprised himself with his words. He hadn't meant to sound so desperate for Joseph, but if he was being honest with himself, it was the truth. The reality that Joseph might meet someone else, someone closer to his age and where he lived, tore at Stephen's heart. But he was willing to take the chance that it would all work out.

Part of him understood that he wasn't simply falling in love with Joseph, but that he might've already fallen.

Joseph peppered Stephen's face and neck with kisses. "Thank you, Stephen. Thank you for not giving up on me."

Stephen clutched Joseph to his chest. He had to have faith. If they were to make a relationship work under such trying circumstances, Stephen needed to remain strong for them both.

* * *

After Stephen dropped him off at the corner by the military housing, he noticed how Stephen had waited to make sure that he made it inside.

I can't believe how fucking safe I feel with him.

Joseph knew he was falling in love with Stephen but didn't dare say anything. He didn't want the older man to think he was just an immature, overly emotional kid. Maybe after they'd been together a little longer, he could share those feelings with him. He didn't want to consider the possibility that Stephen might get tired of waiting for them to be together.

He lay back on his bed once more, less than forty-eight hours left until he'd be leaving Nogales. Gone from where the man he cared about more than anything lived. Joseph rolled on his side and punched his pillow. It was such bullshit. He finally had a chance at some happiness, and it seemed as if it was being ripped away from him.

Still, he had to have faith. Faith in the connection they shared. Stephen was already working on them getting together in a couple of weeks since he'd likely have Rigo back on duty with him by then.

In some ways, it had worked out for the best. Now he'd

have a chance to spend some time with his mom. He still hadn't told her how he'd been placed on unpaid leave. He'd decided he could wait and deal with her hysterical reaction in person.

Sighing, he tried to force himself to get some sleep. After a very long while, he drifted off, the look on Stephen's face as he'd come with him earlier still etched clearly in his mind.

* * *

Stephen sat in one of the uniquely uncomfortable hospital chairs next to Rigo's bed. His partner was still asleep, and Stephen was waiting for him to wake up so they could discuss the latest info on the case.

Joseph had left Nogales that morning and Stephen was extra cranky. They'd only been able to say a quick goodbye over the phone. He tried to keep his focus more on drug cartels and potential informers and less on Joseph's beautiful cock and ass. He squirmed and mumbled some curses.

"You look like you're doing the potty dance over there. Everything all right?"

Stephen scowled at the now very much awake Rigo. "I thought you were asleep."

"I was faking it, but I got tired of waiting for you to leave."

"They didn't tell you? I'm moving in."

"Won't your boyfriend be jealous?"

Stephen pressed his lips together.

This is fucked. The kid's been gone an hour and I'm already a mess.

Rigo arched his eyebrows. "Ah, there's a story, I see. I'm bored out of my skull over here. Out with it."

"Well, I never had the chance to tell you—what with you having the audacity to get shot and all—but we did get together that night."

Guarded Desires

"And?"

"Oh, I could tell you, but I have a digital recording of the whole thing. Came out quite nice, I especially like the light as it bounces off Joseph's shapely—"

"That's enough. You win the first round of the sarcasm wars. Can I assume you guys are an item now?"

Stephen tried to maintain a light-hearted expression. Judging from the look on Rigo's face, he was failing miserably.

"Uh-oh. Should I ask?"

Stephen sighed. "It's not that type of 'uh-oh'."

"I wasn't aware there were different types. What kind is this one?"

"The kind where everything is too wonderful and perfect, but the other person has to leave and go back to Mesa."

"He's not interested in coming to see you?"

"Oh, he's definitely interested. He asked me to wait for him."

"Then why are you being such a dickhole?"

Stephen mock-gasped. "Dickhole? How rude. And that's not the problem. I'd wait forever for him." Stephen cleared his throat as Rigo shot up his eyebrows. "It's this whole mess with the cartel. I can't take any chances with him the same way you can't with Carla and the kids."

"Damn, homey. I didn't even know you were capable of falling in love."

"I didn't *say* I was in love."

"You don't have to say it to be in it."

"Never mind. I don't want to talk about it right now."

"Everyone else I've ever met who's in love gets *less* cranky." Rigo waved his hand around. "Then there's you."

"That's because you bring out my inner hostile man."

"As opposed to the outer one?"

"Okay, okay—you win round two. While you've been lying

147

around all day and slacking off on the job, have you come up with any ideas on who our mole might be?"

"Or how many."

Stephen straightened in the lumpy chair. "You think there's more than one?"

It would explain why different locations had been compromised at different times.

Rigo motioned for Stephen to get closer. He dragged the obnoxious chair over to Rigo's bed, the thick curved legs scraping loudly on the floor. Rigo glared at him.

"Don't you lift large metal objects when you're building all those He-Man muscles? That chair too heavy for you?"

"Focus, Rigo. Multiple informers?"

Rigo leaned in closer. "Think about it. Antonio knew to head straight for you the minute he exited the tunnel. He knew you were already out there and in what direction. The guys at the drug buy knew I was a fake. Agent Spender, the other men out there, and finally, the last hit."

"But we agreed it was more of a diversionary tactic than anything."

"Diverting from what? The only thing I can't put together right now is why they specifically asked for you and me that night. We never made it there because we caught on, so it almost makes me wonder if the entire plan didn't work out the way they'd wanted."

Stephen mulled over what Rigo said. "Or maybe it did. There's another thing that's been bugging me this whole time. If the diversion was meant to leave the Nogales main crossing vulnerable, what was the purpose of that? To waste a bunch of people? How does that keep their product moving back and forth?"

"To instill more fear? It certainly achieved that."

"Scaring the crap out of people is awesome, I agree. But at

some point, actually need to make a gazillion dollars selling drugs. And you can't do that unless you get the product to the customers."

He'd missed the back and forth with Rigo. They were always able to come up with more effective theories that way.

"True." Rigo rubbed his chin. "Okay, if we go back to that night when the border exploded, what do we think really went on? If you were a heinous drug dealer, why would you have done that?"

Stephen's stomach clenched. "Oh shit."

"Could you expand on that theory a bit?"

Stephen brought his voice lower. "It would sort of be like a double cross. Remember how we thought it was too obvious, too easy. What did you say—like they sent out party invitations?"

"Yeah. And?"

"They *knew* we'd figure it out. They weren't trying to divert us from the Nogales main border crossing. They were trying to divert us from the new *tunnels* at the other location."

Realization slowly spread across Rigo's face. "Holy fucking shit. I think you're right." He grunted. "And that hardly ever happens."

"They could've brought in a fuckload of product that night through those other tunnels while half the Guard and all the DEA and border agents were playing *Call of Duty* at the main crossing."

"How do we prove it?"

Stephen pressed his lips together. "We need to get back out there. Find the locations of those tunnels, then set up a secret operation to catch them on the move."

Rigo groaned. "Come on, homey. Have you ever met Boyd? He's been cock-blocking us this entire time."

Stephen's blood chilled. He put his finger to his lips then

stood. Checking the hallway while still concealing himself behind the threshold of Rigo's room, he pulled the door shut. He continued to indicate to Rigo to keep quiet.

"You're right, Rigo, he'll never go for it. And anyway, it's a wild theory. I probably haven't been getting enough sleep. Let's try and brainstorm some more."

Stephen picked up a small notepad and pencil from inside Rigo's hospital end stand drawer. He scribbled a message on the pad then held it up for Rigo to read.

"*I think Boyd is the mole. The room might be bugged.*"

Rigo coughed loudly, nodding, his eyes wide.

"Here buddy, let me grab you some water."

Stephen turned on the tap then shuffled back to Rigo, whispering in his ear, "I'm going to tear this rat down. You get better fast so we can take turns drop-kicking his ass across Arizona. I'm headed back to the office. I'll keep you informed somehow. Do *not* let Carla and the kids come back."

Rigo nodded again, and Stephen shut off the water.

Stephen let out a dramatic yawn. "Well, I'd better get going. I have some errands to run, then I should head into the office, see if anything new is happening there."

"Yeah, thanks for stopping by, homey. Talk to you later."

Stephen gave Rigo a thumbs-up and hurried out of the room. He needed to get a hold of Joseph and make sure he was all right. If Boyd really was the mole and he'd been recording his and Rigo's conversations, he might know all about Joseph. He might know a lot more than they even realized.

His gut instinct was working overtime and none of what it told him was good.

* * *

Guarded Desires

"Mom, stop crying. It's not as bad as it sounds. Mr. Wilkinson said I could come back any time."

"They're not going to dishonorably discharge you?" Joseph's mom sniffled into a tissue, her eyes red and swollen from when she'd burst into tears after Joseph had told her of his punishment.

Joseph took a deep breath. "Mom. I already told you. It's unpaid leave, that's it."

He didn't dare tell her the part where he was court-martialed, she'd come unglued. As it was, he'd only been back in Mesa for a couple of hours, his mom was hysterical, and his heart ached for Stephen.

He'd been so hopeful when Stephen had talked of being willing to do that with his former boyfriend. That made it seem as though it was a doable option. Maybe it was that way from Stephen's point of view, but he wasn't sure he could take it. He missed him way too much already.

Joseph found himself playing everything Stephen had said to him over and over in his mind. That he would wait for him. How much he cared about him. That he would do whatever it took for them to be together. A satisfied smile spread across Joseph's face as he remembered his Stephen's words.

His mother grunted, bringing Joseph back to the present. "I've never seen anyone so happy to be destroying their lives."

"Jesus, Mom. I'm not destroying anything."

"Don't you curse! I did not raise you like that."

Joseph dragged a hand across the top of his head. "I know Mom, sorry. Let me go put my stuff away."

She'd divorced his dad when he and his sister had been very young, and she'd tried very hard to instill strong moral values in them. She was a hard-working woman who had waitressed for many years, then got a degree to do medical billing. Now she was able to work out of an office and be off her feet.

Since his sister had married and moved to the Midwest, Joseph was all she had. He felt a strong sense of responsibility toward her.

He had told his sister he was gay when he had only been twelve years old, and she'd promptly told their mom. She'd cried then, too. She claimed it had to do with him not being able to carry on the Pirelli name. It seemed like a lame excuse. She couldn't stand the Pirellis—his father in particular.

However, she'd never stopped loving or caring about him. But they certainly never discussed his orientation. The two years with Dorian had been very hard on her. She hadn't been able to understand why he could never come and visit, or why she couldn't visit him.

When she'd found out about the abuse later after the DEA had stepped in, it somehow confirmed her theory that all those bad things happened to him because he was gay. He'd been so angry with her about that for a while, but had eventually realized that whatever guilt she carried over not being able to protect or help him had probably been what caused her to act like that.

The house phone rang, and he hurried to answer it. Maybe it was Mr. Wilkinson returning his call. Having somewhere to go everyday would help the time to pass faster until he could see Stephen again. He reached the kitchen counter where the phone was cradled.

"Hello?"

"Hi bitch. Miss me?"

Joseph's legs gave way and he crumpled to the ground.

It can't be. Dorian's in prison. Isn't he?

* * *

Guarded Desires

Frantically searching every file he had on the Vasquez cartel and re-examining every dead lead, Stephen's gut told him there had to be something he was missing—something that could tie Boyd in with the whole mess. His gut instinct was on high alert and even though he had no proof, he was certain his boss was involved. But the question remained—how involved, and at what level?

The office was quiet, however, he still didn't trust that he might not be heard if he made any calls—disposable cell or not. If there was a bug at his or Rigo's desk, it wouldn't matter how many untraceable phones they had.

Stephen gathered a few numbers together and thought he'd head down the street to a coffeehouse with outdoor seating. He could make a few inquiries by phone there without the worry of being overhead.

And I can have a chance to hear Joseph's sweet voice.

After making his way to the coffee place, he ordered an Americano, then took a seat outside. He made sure to sit as far away from everyone else as possible. Since it was midday, the place wasn't that crowded.

His first call was to Joseph. Not the most professional move, although if he could speak with him for a few moments, he might be able to concentrate better on everything else going on. The ring kept going and going until the voicemail came on.

Dammit.

"Joseph, it's Stephen. I was just checking in, seeing how it's all going at home. Hope your mom's doing well. Call when you can. Miss you."

Stephen sighed. He'd really wanted to talk to him, but that was always the challenge of long-distance relationships. They would both have other obligations, other things going on. Stephen certainly didn't expect the young man to be sitting around all day waiting for Stephen to call. He'd try him again later.

After he'd made a few more calls, his burner phone vibrated. His heart leaped. Hopefully, it was Joseph getting back to him. However, the hospital line was what popped up on the screen. Only Rigo and Joseph had his disposable cell number.

"Rigo?"

"Homey, you need to get back down here. There was a bunch of commotion a little while ago, and I just overheard one of the nurses say that Sanchez was found dead in his room."

"*What?*"

"Yeah. And can I confess something to you?"

"Of course."

"I'm worried I might be next on the elimination list."

* * *

Joseph had no choice.

Fuck. I told myself I'd never, ever be in this position again.

But that was before Dorian escaped from prison. Joseph was furious that he hadn't been warned. Owing to the circumstances of his relationship with his sadistic ex, the authorities were supposed to notify Joseph of any changes in Dorian's incarceration. He couldn't think of any bigger change than Dorian busting out.

He sat perched at the edge of his bed, rubbing his clammy, sweaty palms across the tops of his denim-clad legs. His heart thundered, as if it had climbed into his throat. It didn't seem as though he could take a full breath and dizziness threatened.

He'd never been so fucking terrified.

"*Wait for me there, bitch. I'll honk three times, and if you're*

Guarded Desires

not outside and in my car within sixty seconds, I'll introduce myself to your mom by slitting her throat."

Bile rose into his throat, and he was in danger of heaving. Dorian had also warned him against contacting the authorities. He claimed to have someone ready to take out Stephen if he did.

How the fuck does he know about Stephen?

He couldn't piece the puzzle together. As much as the entire thing thrust him back to that place where Dorian wanted to own him, control him, abuse him—he sensed something was off.

If Antonio had been part of the drug cartel that Stephen and Rigo were working so hard to take down, was it that much of a stretch to think that Dorian played a part in all of it too? Joseph had the awful feeling that he might only be a pawn to get to Stephen.

Joseph glanced down at his cell phone. When Stephen called five minutes ago, all he could do was stare at it helplessly. He'd ached to be able to pick it up, to hear Stephen's voice one more time. But he didn't dare. Not if he wanted to keep Stephen safe.

He knew he wouldn't survive whatever it was Dorian had planned for him. He had no delusions that the psychopath cared about him in any way other than as someone he could use to satisfy his twisted desires. Back when he'd been so helpless and in Dorian's clutches, he'd given in to the inevitability that he'd die by Dorian's hand one day.

Then the DEA rescued him and with determination, he'd risen above all the shit from his time with Dorian and become strong. Now, he only needed to be strong for a little while longer. Just long enough so he could somehow make sure Stephen was safe.

Three honks sounded from outside and Joseph yelped. He

sucked in a deep breath as he pushed up from the bed with trembling hands, forcing his wobbly legs to move toward the front door and to his doom.

It no longer mattered what happened to him as long as his family and Stephen were safe.

Chapter Twelve

When Stephen arrived at the hospital, it was already clogged with reporters, law enforcement and CBP agents. There was so much confusion, and Stephen was so anxious about what Rigo had said on the phone, that he headed straight for his partner's room.

Rigo threw his hands in there as Stephen entered his room. "Homey, the fuck? Where you been? It's like a madhouse in here."

"No kidding. Before I go and stick my nose in it, you get any updates?"

Rigo shook his head. "All I know is that when the nurse was making her rounds, she found Hank dead."

Stephen frowned. "Didn't he have a guard posted outside his room, too?"

"That's why you've got to get me *out* of here. The so-called guard was taking a break when it happened."

Stephen set his mouth in a grim line. "And it's definite that Hank was taken out, that he didn't die from his injuries?"

"How the fuck should I know? You're the guy with the legs

Morticia Knight

who can walk around. I didn't drag you back down here so soon for your charming company."

Stephen growled in frustration. He doubted anyone would make a move on Rigo with so much activity going on at the hospital, but everything kept taking unexpected left turns. He didn't want to make any rash assumptions.

"I'm going to go see what I can find out, and then we're going to use this clusterfuck to our advantage."

"Huh?"

Stephen leaned down, sliding his Glock under the covers of Rigo's bed as he did. "Keep watch with this and be ready. As soon as I come back, we're leaving together."

Rigo whispered next to his ear, "Can you toss me my *chones* or something? I don't need my junk flapping all around Nogales."

Stephen went to the cubby where Rigo's clothing had been stuffed into a large plastic hospital bag then pulled out his briefs. The bloody jeans had been discarded.

Flinging Rigo his underwear, he commented, "Trust me. I wouldn't put the fine citizens of Nogales through that torture. I'll be right back."

After rushing out of the door, he headed down the hall where Sanchez's room had been. The majority of people were in that area, and Stephen hoped he could subtly glean some information about what had happened before sneaking Rigo out of the hospital.

"Agent Morris. I see your partner must've alerted you to this unexpected development."

Stephen whirled around at the sound of Boyd's voice. He kept his expression impassive. "Yes, this is such a shock. You both survived that attack at the border, then Hank is killed here at the hospital." Stephen pressed his lips together, shaking his head as if it were all so horrible. "I

158

Guarded Desires

imagine you'll have extra security for yourself after this tragic event."

Boyd narrowed his eyes as he regarded Stephen. "Killed? Why did you phrase it that way?"

Stephen arched his eyebrows as if he were utterly confused. "Oh? Did get the wrong intel? I heard some officers over there..." He indicated down the hall where several groups of people were clustered, then tilted his head. "Huh. They were there a minute ago." He glanced back at Boyd. "I'm sure they're around here somewhere. But anyway, they were discussing that it seemed as if Hank's death was a professional hit, that he must've known something."

Boyd's gaze remained unwavering as he considered Stephen. After a moment he spoke. "That's an interesting theory. You should probably look into it."

"I certainly will."

"I think we've done everything we can here." Boyd crossed his arms. "I have to give a press conference in a few minutes. Then, I have a lead of my own on the Vasquez cartel that I need to follow-up on."

Stephen rubbed his hands together. "Excellent. When can I hear about it?"

The slightest hint of a smile curled one side of Boyd's mouth. "You'll hear about it soon enough. If you'll excuse me?"

Stephen watched as his boss strolled down the hall, no hurry to his stride, the picture of a man in complete control. His boss' odd demeanor nagged at the corners of his mind, but he pushed it aside for the time being.

He had a difficult choice to make. He could try and nose around about Sanchez some more, or he could use the few minutes when Boyd would be distracted by the press conference to get Rigo out of the hospital undetected.

His concern for Rigo won out.

159

Stephen jogged down to Rigo's room. Now that Boyd was out of the way, everyone else—including the staff—still seemed sufficiently occupied. They might not pay any attention to what Stephen and Rigo were doing. As he passed an empty wheelchair, he grabbed it, rolling it ahead of him. He pushed into Rigo's room with the chair.

"Your taxi has arrived. Where to? Vegas? Grand Canyon?"

"Wherever you're not going. Any hope of me getting some pants?"

Stephen reached behind Rigo with one arm, grasping him under his legs with the other, then lifted him out of bed.

"Whoa there, Tarzan. Get your beefy mitts off me."

Stephen ignored his partner and hoisted him up, carrying him to the chair. Rigo tried to wriggle free but howled in pain from the wound in his leg. Stephen lowered him onto the wheelchair.

"Shut up, you idiot. We're trying *not* to attract attention."

"I feel like Scarlett O'Hara right now, except you ain't no Clark Gable."

"Damn straight. I'm much sexier. Now be a good boy and I'll get you a blankie to cover your legs."

As usual, Rigo's answer involved the use of his middle finger.

After Stephen had his partner situated, he checked the hallways. Once he felt it was clear, he rolled Rigo out of the room and, with a steady pace, headed toward the back elevators that was for staff only. Unfortunately, he discovered he'd need to have a special key to activate them.

Dammit.

The doors slid open and without making any eye contact with the nurse exiting, he rolled Rigo in.

"Hey, this is for hospital personnel only!"

"Yes, I know." He held out his badge. "This man is in

danger. He's a crucial witness and it's vital that I remove from the hospital immediately after the recent incident."

The kid paled. "Oh, of course. But you'll need the key to operate this thing. Here. I'll take you."

Once they'd been escorted safely from the hospital and Stephen loaded Rigo into his car, they had to plan their next move. But Rigo couldn't let their whole daring escape go by without comment.

"You sure know how to sweet-talk the young boys. Did you see how he was batting his eyelashes at you?"

"He told me before he left that he's always wanted a three-some with a hot hunk and a cranky DEA agent in a wheelchair."

"That's silly. You weren't even in a wheelchair."

Stephen rolled his eyes. "Ideas?"

"Did you take the Honda to the house and put it in the garage?"

"I sold it on eBay, but the bidder backed out. So I decided to let you keep it."

Rigo let out a dramatic sigh. "Thank God for flakes on the internet. I say we grab it and head out to the tunnels."

"What about your leg? Plus, if you're going to wear a dress in public, I can find you something much more flattering than that hospital couture you're rocking right now."

"I don't think any of your clothes will fit me."

Stephen's disposable cell vibrated. He grabbed it from his blazer pocket and noted the call was from Joseph. He was torn. First, he checked the mirrors to see if anyone was around, then signaled and pulled to the side of the road.

"Do you think anyone followed us?"

Rigo shook his head. "While you've been fretting over my wardrobe, I've been keeping an eye out. We're good."

Stephen pressed the answer button. "Hey, babe. Thanks for calling."

"You're welcome, asshole. All the same, I don't think we know each other well enough yet for pet names. But I *do* know your little bitch of a boyfriend *real* good. We used to have lots of fun together. Right, Joseph?"

All the air left Stephen's body and his stomach lurched. A loud smack sounded, quickly followed by Joseph's agonized cries. Stephen was vaguely aware of Rigo's hand on his arm. A rage he'd never known existed inside him boiled to the surface.

"I am going to fucking *kill* you," Stephen's growled out.

"Not before I've crushed Joseph with my bare hands. His own mother won't be able to recognize him after I'm done. So, you're going to shut the fuck up and listen to me very carefully. I'm a fairly reasonable guy once you get to know me. Bring that crippled partner of yours along with your sorry ass to Phoenix. You have three hours to get here. You're going to wait for my call, and we'll set up a meeting place. It should be obvious, but let me reiterate it to you—if you contact the DEA, police or CBP—I *will* know about it. I will cut off a piece of Joseph's body, take a photograph and send it to you if you do not follow my instructions. We will keep trying until you meet with us alone or there's nothing left to slice off of Joseph—whichever comes first."

Sounds of hideous laughter echoed on the line and Stephen gripped the phone so hard he was afraid he might crush it.

"What is this all about Dorian? What do you *want*?"

Joseph yelled in the background, "Don't, Stephen! It's a trap! I don't want you to—!"

Stephen flinched at the sound of another brutal smack.

"Shut up, you piece of shit!"

Be quiet Joseph, don't fight him. I'm coming for you.

"Listen fuckhead," continued Dorian. "My people want

Guarded Desires

you and your partner. That's it. You come here alone, and your used up piece of ass goes free, we don't—ow, *fuck!* I told you assholes to hold him down. He fucking bit me!"

It sounded as if Joseph were being hit with something.

Oh God, no. Not the belt.

"*Stop it!* Stop it now or I won't come. There's no point if he's dead."

"Oh, you'll come, won't he, Joseph?"

He heard choking, like Joseph was being strangled.

"*Won't* he, Joseph?"

Moaning and in obvious pain, Joseph spoke with a cracked voice. "Don't Stephen, they'll kill you, please don't—"

There was another loud smack and Stephen's heart shattered.

"Three hours, asshole. You'll get my next instructions then."

Then the phone went dead.

* * *

Rages and temper tantrums were not something that usually grabbed a hold of Stephen. He took everything that came at him in life and considered how to best deal with it from a place of calm and determination. His sense of humor had always been a way of deflecting some of the more troubling things he had to deal with, especially in his line of work.

But he'd come completely unglued after hearing Joseph's suffering on the other end of the line. He'd stood outside of the car by the side of the road, screaming and bashing the vehicle for at least ten minutes before Rigo had calmly reminded him that they needed to head to Phoenix immediately. That statement had struck Stephen square in the chest.

Rigo knows the danger, yet he's still willing to take the risk.

They'd been driving in silence for almost half an hour, the grim reality of what they faced weighing heavily on them.

"I can still drop you off somewhere. I'll be taking you to your death sentence. What about Carla and the kids?"

"Don't write me off so quick, homey. There's a way around this. We still have a couple hours to untangle this mess, run possible scenarios."

Stephen drove with one hand on the wheel. He leaned his elbow on the armrest of the black SUV and chewed on the tip of his thumb. His emotions were too caught up in what Joseph was suffering through, and he knew he wasn't thinking straight.

Exactly what they'd counted on.

What they didn't realize was that Rigo was his secret weapon. Their synergy was something he'd never experienced with another partner before. That alone made them an almost unstoppable force in working investigations.

"Hit me with something, Rigo, I need some hope here."

"That's my boy. All right, this is what we know so far. Boyd's a dickhead—no surprise there. Obviously, he's our mole. But we have to assume there are more since that Dorian character mentioned they would know if the police or CBP were notified in addition to the DEA."

Stephen glanced sideways at his partner. "Or he's lying."

"Or he's lying. But I don't think so. I don't think they'd take that chance. The next question is—who's the one really in charge? Is it Dorian? Boyd? The mysterious Vasquez? Who works for who? We figure *that* out and we'll get closer to what we're up against."

Stephen gasped, straightening in his seat, and gripping the wheel with both hands. "Nothing was said about the Guard."

Rigo whistled. "Holy shit."

Stephen sped up the truck.

It's time to pay the Mesa Armory a little visit.

Guarded Desires

* * *

Joseph spit out blood onto the cement floor where he was chained to a metal pipe. His bottom teeth had sliced right through his lip when Dorian had backhanded him particularly hard, and he couldn't get the bleeding to stop. Not that it really mattered. He'd known he was going to die from the moment he heard Dorian's voice on the phone. But that knowledge had been sadly reinforced once Dorian didn't even attempt to conceal where he was taking him.

It was hot enough outside that the cold floor didn't bother him all that much in the basement of the large carpet manufacturing warehouse. The business was obviously a front for the cartel in some way. Everything was connected. Antonio, Dorian, him—and now Stephen and Rigo.

Dorian was too stupid and volatile to be the leader of such a large and successful operation as the Vasquez cartel. Plainly, his abuser was being used to lure Stephen and his Stephen's partner to their deaths.

Please Stephen, stay away. Don't risk it.

He put every ounce of himself into praying that Stephen wouldn't come to his rescue, yet realized it was pointless. He'd never been so sure of someone's love for him. He didn't even know how he could know such a thing, just that he did. All the worry and anxiety over trying to make a long-distance relationship work seemed so silly and petty all of a sudden. Now that they were faced with losing their lives, Joseph would give anything to have the chance to tell Stephen that he loved him.

And if there was any way he could manage it, take Dorian with him when he was taken out.

There was no doubt in his mind that he was already dead, but it didn't mean there wasn't a way to work it so that Dorian ate it, too. It would almost be worth losing his life so the piece of filth would no longer be roaming the earth.

The chain attached to the metal cuff on his ankle was something he would never be able to break free from. However, to achieve his objective, he didn't need to. All he had to do was get Dorian close enough so he could kick his feet out from under him like he'd learned in kickboxing, knock him to the ground then strangle him with the chain.

However, he would need to be quick and use his strength to hopefully snap the psycho's neck before Dorian realized what was happening. It would be difficult because Dorian always made sure he was surrounded by reinforcements, which meant Joseph had to finish him off before he was stopped.

The stairs leading down to his prison room creaked under the weight of descending footsteps. It was about ten by twenty, and he assumed it was some sort of utility area. Other than the inexplicable mattress in the corner, the rest of the area contained tools, cleaning supplies, a couple of vacuums and haphazardly stacked boxes.

Dorian appeared at the bottom of the stairs.

Joseph swallowed hard. *He's alone.*

The unexpected turn of events could be good or could be bad. It would be easier to take Dorian down if no one was around to save him, but he might also have other devious intentions that could thwart Joseph's plan.

Dorian's massive frame filled the opening that led to the stairs. If Dorian and Stephen were to go hand to hand, it would be too close to call.

Joseph winced. He didn't want to think about Stephen—especially not with Dorian in mind. Other than their builds, they were so completely different. Not only in looks—Dorian had longer, blond hair that hung in strings down to his shoulders and he was clean shaven. His expression remained in an

Guarded Desires

almost permanent scowl that marred what should've been a very handsome face.

And the brute had no heart. No soul. Stephen was everything that Dorian could never hope to be.

"How's my little bitch doing?"

His body rumbled with what Joseph guessed was supposed to be laughter. He also stayed just out of range for Joseph's plan. Still, he paced as he spoke, and Joseph was hopeful.

"You know, your DEA scum boyfriend and his partner will be dead soon and I was thinking—what's going to happen to poor, useless Joseph? Because he'll have to die, too." Dorian tapped his chin with one finger. "Unless I can come up with a reason to keep him around."

It was unnerving to hear Dorian talk about him in third person. He'd always been sadistic and prone to odd ravings, but he seemed even more unhinged than Joseph remembered.

Or maybe I'm not as accustomed to crazy anymore. I know what goodness is.

Dorian regarded him with a maniacal grin. "What do you think we should do, huh? You're no longer as pure as when I had you. That fucking agent's been inside you. You're used goods." Dorian spit on the floor. "But it might be fun to keep you around to be everyone's entertainment, put on a good show. How does that sound?"

Joseph fixed him with a glare. "I'd rather be dead a thousand times over than have you or any of your goons touch me, you disgusting piece of dog shit."

Dorian's jaw dropped and his expression radiated shock as if he'd been slapped. Scarlet red crept up his neck and into his face, his muscular biceps bunching up as he clenched his fists. Joseph figured this would probably be it. Dorian would beat him to a pulp.

167

"I am going to rip your fucking guts out..." He advanced toward Joseph.

That's it. Just a little closer...

A loud boom shook the building so hard it actually caused Dorian to lose his balance. Dust and bits of cement pieces scattered on the floor. Gunfire erupted upstairs and Dorian's jaw went slack again, his eyes bulging, his head whipping around as if he were trying to grasp what was going on.

It's disbelief.

Dorian glare at Joseph. "If that's your boyfriend trying to save your ugly ass, he's going to have a big surprise when he gets down here and all that's left is a bloody pile of broken bones."

As Dorian moved closer, Joseph prepared himself to follow through with his plan. He gritted his teeth and right as Dorian reached him, Joseph shot out the leg that wasn't chained. He was able to swipe it and knock Dorian off his feet, Joseph rolling out of the way as Dorian came down hard, almost crushing him. Joseph swiftly grabbed the chain, clutching it tightly with his fists. Then he flung the chain around Dorian's neck before his abuser could catch his breath.

Joseph yanked on the chain with all his might. It was obvious that Dorian hadn't expected Joseph to fight back, to have become stronger. But as he'd always feared, he could never be a physical match for someone of Dorian's size. Even with all his physical training, Joseph's muscles shook with the effort of cutting off the airway in Dorian's massive neck. The behemoth of a man regained enough awareness that he reached up to grasp Josephs forearms. His thick, strong fingers dug into Joseph's skin, squeezing so hard Joseph was sure his bones would snap.

The struggle seemed to be captured in infinity, but it couldn't have been going on for more than thirty seconds. All the while they fought to the death, the thundering reports of a gun battle carried on overhead. Overwhelming pain built in Joseph's arms as the pressure from Dorian's crushing grip threatened to weaken him.

"No! Let him go!"

Joseph was so startled to hear Stephen's voice that he did just that. As soon as he loosened his hold, Dorian took the opportunity to flip Joseph over his head. He slammed Joseph down hard on his back, but the majority of his body landed on the thin mattress that was nearby.

Gasping for air, he rolled on his side and saw Dorian and Stephen battling one another, fists flying, punches landing. They were both out of Joseph's reach and he was filled with terror. The men snarled and growled while Joseph watched the brutal battle, wishing he could help Stephen instead of being imprisoned by the chain.

Stephen slammed into Dorian and his foot slid behind him just far enough for Joseph to grab his ankle and hold on. The move distracted Dorian enough that Stephen was able to land a solid punch to his face. He hammered Dorian repeatedly with his fist, but then Dorian flung his arms up in a wide arc and head-butted Stephen.

Stephen lost his balance, falling backwards, far from where Joseph lay. He observed in helpless frustration as Dorian crouched over him, took Stephen's head between his hands then bashed it against the cement floor.

"No!"

Joseph launched himself toward the horrific scene, but the chain yanked him back. Stephen clasped his hands around Dorian's wrists, fighting against the attempts by the psycho to continually bang his skull on the ground.

"Stop!"

Yelling was pointless, but Joseph didn't know what else to

do. Tears spilled down his cheeks as Dorian slid his hands around Stephen's throat and bore down. Dorian straddled his chest, Stephen's face turning bright red, his tongue poking out of his mouth as he struggled for air.

He's going to die. Oh God, no.

"Help! We need help down here—someone help!"

Dorian kept one meaty paw on Stephen's larynx and used the other to reach inside his torn blazer. Joseph heard the same rumbling from him as he had earlier—Dorian's twisted version of laughter. Sheer horror tore through Joseph as Dorian pulled out a small pistol and waved it around.

"As fun as this has been, I'm tired of playing with you." Dorian glared over his shoulder at Joseph. "Say goodbye to your boyfriend!"

A shot rang out, hitting Dorian right between the eyes. Joseph gasped as Dorian fell back in a heap, Stephen rolling out from under him, choking and gasping for air. Joseph gazed up in gratitude at the Guardsman holding the rifle that had taken Dorian out.

Harrison.

Chapter Thirteen

The term 'a pounding headache' took on new meaning for Stephen. He lay on a gurney, being poked and prodded by a rather attractive young medic. But the only man he ever wanted to poke or prod him again was Joseph, and if someone didn't tell him where he was and how he was doing immediately, he was going to have to start kicking ass all over again.

"Ow! Was that necessary?"

"Sorry, sir." The medic smiled down at him. "It looks like you might have a cracked rib. And your head should be examined."

"I've been telling him that for years, but he simply won't listen."

Stephen turned to see Rigo rolling up to him in the wheelchair they'd stolen from the Nogales hospital.

"Don't fuck with me now, Rigo. Where the hell is Joseph?"

"Does that imply that I can fuck with you later?"

"I swear to all that is holy..."

"Relax dumbass, he's over by the other ambulance whining

about your sorry behind. I can't imagine what he sees in you. Love is so perplexing."

Stephen raised himself up from the gurney, wincing in pain. The twinky medic pushed uselessly against Stephen's chest to stop him.

Rigo snorted. "Yeah, good luck with that. Bigfoot always gets his way."

Stephen flipped Rigo the bird. All was back to normal.

Clutching his side and gritting his teeth, Stephen limped over to the vehicle where Joseph was. His sweetheart sat on the edge of a gurney with his back to Stephen. Another medic was in the process of trying to encourage him to lie down, but Joseph kept shoving the man's hands off him and yelling.

"Why aren't you *listening* to me? I'm not fucking going anywhere until you tell me where Agent Morris is. I have to make sure he's all right!"

"I'm all right now that you're here, babe."

Joseph leaped off the gurney, whipping his head around until his gaze landed on him. It looked as though he were trying to say something, but couldn't form any words. Stephen held his arms open, the invitation he'd become used to giving Joseph. He took a hurried step as if to rush toward him, but stumbled. Stephen lurched forward at the same time as the medic, catching Joseph before he fell.

Despite how much his body hurt, he held Joseph close, Joseph hugging him back, his head resting against Stephen's chest. Stephen looked down at Joseph's ankle and saw the angry red and purple mark. There was a gash where the metal had worn away the skin, and it appeared as if the medic had been in the process of cleaning it before Stephen interrupted him.

Stephen whispered to Joseph. "Come on, babe. Let's get you taken care of."

Guarded Desires

Joseph shook his head, still hanging on to Stephen. "I can't let you go. I won't let anyone take you away from me."

Stephen could only imagine the new traumas that would plague the young man after his most recent ordeal. But Stephen knew that no matter what had happened, he would stay by the man he loved and help him through it.

"I'm right here, I'm not going anywhere."

He took Joseph's hand and led him to the gurney. As soon as he had Joseph lying on it with his ankle propped up, he was able to really examine him and see the damage Dorian had inflicted.

Joseph's bottom lip was puffy, and it appeared it had been cut. Bruises were forming on both sides of his face, and a long scratch trailed along his cheek. When they were alone later, he would ask Joseph what had happened, but not in front of strangers. All that mattered right then was getting Joseph medical attention.

He spoke close to Joseph's ear. "You have to tell the doctor anything that was done to hurt you, even if it might be embarrassing. I want to make sure you're taken care of."

Joseph took Stephen's hand and leaned in. "Don't worry, he didn't do that to me. Just the belt..."

Stephen closed his eyes and squeezed Joseph's hand, swallowing around a lump in his throat. "He can never hurt you again, babe."

Joseph peered up at him, tears in his eyes. "I know."

Stephen's eye burned as well. "I don't care how it happens, but you're going to be with me from now on. I'm not leaving you alone."

Joseph's lips curled into a small smile. "Promise?"

"Promise." Stephen smiled back, but immediately regretted it. Dorian had landed a good punch on his cheek, and it was killing him.

Joseph's expression radiated worry, and Stephen shook his head. "I'm okay."

Joseph frowned and started climbing off the gurney. Stephen clutched his hand tighter, not letting him go any farther.

"What the hell are you doing? Get back up there."

"Not until you get checked out. I'm serious." Joseph glanced around until he spotted the medic from the other ambulance. "Excuse me. Medic? This man needs help. He said he feels really dizzy and might pass out."

Stephen snorted a laugh. "Troublemaker."

Epilogue

A month had passed since the terrifying episode with Dorian. So much was revealed about the cartel that it made Joseph's head spin. As he'd only ever been on the periphery of the investigation, he could only imagine how Stephen and Rigo felt about everything.

The most shocking thing that had been divulged was that Special Agent in Charge Boyd had been more than just a mole —he'd also been the elusive and mysterious Vasquez. He'd spent years building the drug ring, recruiting people as he went along. Antonio and Dorian had been associates with him from early on.

It took some creative use of his thug contacts, but Boyd had managed to help both criminals to escape. With all the people he'd placed in various agencies—from the prisons to law enforcement to CBP to the DEA—he'd been able to control and keep track of everything going on around him. Even Hank Sanchez, someone Rigo said he'd known for years, had been on Boyd's payroll. When Boyd worried that Hank might talk, he'd been disposed of.

Morticia Knight

As Boyd became a bigger force in the illegal drug industry, and the operation more sophisticated, his greed and sense of invulnerability is what brought him down. Unbeknownst to him—and even Rigo and Stephen—the FBI and Homeland Security had been conducting their own investigation. Their search had led them to the Nogales DEA office, but they couldn't determine who the man behind the mask was.

The other thing Boyd hadn't counted on was Stephen and Rigo's relentless pursuit of finding the truth, or that the one entity he didn't have in his pocket—the National Guard—would be integral in helping to free Joseph and bring the whole operation to its knees.

When a frantic Stephen and Rigo had showed up at the Mesa Armory with their wild story, a quick phone call to Homeland Security was all the Guard had needed to get the okay to move in on the cartel at the carpet warehouse. In addition to Dorian, Boyd had been taken out by a Guardsman. The entire organization crumbled after that day, and hundreds of arrests had been made. Luckily, Boyd had kept meticulous records.

But that was all over with, and finally Joseph felt as if he was truly free. Summer had arrived, and Joseph was enjoying kicking back in a lounge chair in Stephen's yard. They were planning on having Rigo and his family over the next day for a last barbeque before they all picked up and headed to Mesa. Even poor Agent Nelson, who still didn't know he'd been one of Stephen's suspects, was expected to attend.

So much change. All of it wonderful.

Stephen and Rigo had been invited by the Phoenix office of the DEA to transfer over as a team. They'd received accolades for their help in bringing down the Vasquez Cartel, and after very little pondering, both men had jumped at the chance. It would be a salary hike for them, but all Stephen

176

Guarded Desires

could talk about was that he and Joseph would be near one another.

In light of all that happened with the cartel, Joseph's case was reviewed, and he was being taken off suspension the following week. That had also made it easier for him to request permanent orders for the Mesa Armory. He and Stephen would be together—no long-distance relationship.

Stephen from the kitchen after sliding open the glass door, clutching two beers. He approached Joseph and handed him the Bud, then sat down next to him with his Tecate.

"Have you heard from Dan?"

They'd both been pestering Private Harrison to come to the barbeque, Stephen even going so far as to speak with the young man's CO to explain how Dan saved his life. Not that the soldier's Commanding Officer didn't know what had happened, but Stephen thought it might help guarantee that he could join them.

"Yeah. He'll be here early tomorrow. He wants to know if we can find him a date."

Stephen snorted. "I'd offer him Rigo, but I doubt anyone's that hard up. Carla's been begging me to take him off her hands for years."

Laughter spilled from Joseph. Being with Stephen was such a gift. As much as the agent took his job seriously and had been there for Joseph to lean on when night terrors or other issues had plagued him—he was essentially a big, fun-loving teddy bear. He was everything Joseph needed and exactly what he'd always wanted.

Joseph took a sip of his beer. "Oh hey, did I tell you? I finally found out what happened to Private Yuen."

"That's the one who froze up that night in the desert, right?"

"Yeah. Turns out he had some pretty hard core emotional

shit from before he ever even entered the military. But it didn't come to the surface until that night. The whole thing with Spender getting blown away like that was what triggered him."

"He got a medical discharge though, right?"

"Oh yeah. Harrison still stays in contact with him. He's going to school in California somewhere."

"Hmmm."

Joseph noticed that Stephen had finished his beer quickly and was staring at him, a bit of a glimmer in his eyes.

"What?" Joseph chuckled.

"I love the weekends."

Joseph arched his eyebrows. "Okay..."

"I'm tired of all that crap in the house that still needs to be packed up. What about you?"

"Um, what does that have to do with loving weekends?"

"Because here it is, a beautiful day, middle of the afternoon, nowhere to go, you and I alone together... Seems a waste to spend our time wrapping butcher paper around cups and plates."

"Ah, I see." Joseph smiled contentedly. Stephen was still so protective of him, so considerate. He never pressured Joseph sexually. He'd remain playful, suggestive. It was left open for Joseph to respond to him—or not. But as Joseph became more comfortable and secure with Stephen, he'd ended up instigating many of their encounters.

While there was a brief set back after the trauma of being with Dorian, and Stephen had actually gone so far as refusing to wear a belt except when he was at work, Joseph's dedication to leaving his old life behind had kept him going. Stephen's care was a large part of his progress, along with a trauma counselor he'd been seeing.

Just thinking about how considerate Stephen was with him every moment of every day made Joseph's heart swell with love.

Guarded Desires

He needed to say it—to tell Stephen how much he meant to him.

He also wanted to show him. There was absolutely no reason for him to fear or doubt the man who'd risked his life to save him. He wanted their relationship to be complete in all ways. He wanted Stephen to make love to him.

Joseph set down his beer. "Then I think we should go to the bedroom because I want to feel you inside of me. I want you to make me yours."

Stephen's jaw slackened. He dropped to his knees on the grass next to Joseph then gently pulled Joseph off the chair and into his lap.

"Are you sure, babe? I actually enjoy bottoming for you—it's not only because you didn't want me to top you."

Joseph nodded. "I'm very sure. It's important to me for a few reasons. I don't want Dorian to take anything away from me anymore. I want you inside of me—to give myself to you, be claimed by you. I love the way you finger-fuck me, and I know it'll be even more amazing when you fill me completely."

Stephen cradled Joseph's head between his hands and stared directly into his eyes. "It would be my honor then."

Joseph stood, with Stephen doing the same. He offered his hand to Joseph, and they clasped their fingers together, Stephen leading the way to the bedroom. Only the mattress and frame with sheets and a blanket remained. Everything else had already been torn down or packed.

Stephen opened the grooming kit that was on the floor next to the bed. He pulled out a condom and some lube then set them on the mattress. Joseph noted that Stephen seemed more nervous than him.

"This is up to you, babe. How do you want to do this?"

Joseph shook his head. "It's not for me, Stephen. It's for *us*. I love the way you want everything to be just right for me. It means so much how you care about my feelings. But our lovemaking should be about us, not only me. Make love to me the way you would as if nothing bad had ever happened, the way it comes to you naturally." Joseph framed Stephen's face with his palms. "Take me. Fuck me."

Stephen regarded him with a wistful expression. "My sweet Joseph." He swept Joseph up in a fierce embrace then spoke softly into Joseph's ear. "Then you need to know that I love you."

Joseph inhaled sharply. "I love you too, Stephen." He clutched Stephen tighter. "So much. I have for a while but was afraid to tell you."

Stephen pressed a kiss to his temple. "Don't ever be afraid to tell me anything. You're my whole life now."

Joseph buried his face in Stephen's chest. He inhaled Stephen's distinct aroma through his T-shirt but needed to feel the soft fur of his chest against his bare skin.

Stephen stepped back from Joseph a bit. "Let's get rid of these pesky clothes."

Joseph nodded, his small fears giving away to anticipation. He allowed Stephen to take charge, to pull off his clothes, the embarrassment from his scars no longer a concern.

Once Stephen had removed everything, he yanked Joseph to his chest again, using his large hands to knead and stroke every inch of Joseph's body. Stephen flicked his nipples until they peaked, caressed Joseph's throat and tickled his ears. He slipped his fingers in the cleft of Joseph's ass, reaching behind his ball sac to tease him. Then Stephen stroked his lengthening erection. It was as if Stephen was claiming him with his hands alone.

"Lie down."

Joseph's breath hitched a little as he did what he was told.

Guarded Desires

An edge to Stephen's tone emerged that he hadn't heard before. It was darker, sexier. However, Joseph wasn't afraid.

He lay back on the bed, watching as Stephen removed his own clothes while never breaking eye contact. Stephen approached him from the end of the mattress, crawling up the length of his body, placing hungry kisses along the way until he reached Joseph's cock.

Stephen fisted him powerfully at the root of his dick then greedily sucked him into his mouth. Joseph arched his back, a small moan escaping his lips. He clutched at the sheets, his heels digging into the mattress as Stephen sucked him off with complete abandon. He released Joseph's cock, then pushed Joseph's legs back, bending them as much as he could.

Stephen captured one of Joseph's balls between his lips, suckling it gently before taking the other one in. He licked and sucked them, then pried Joseph's ass cheeks apart. Stephen probed his hole with his tongue before plunging it past the tight ring of muscle. Joseph groaned as Stephen tongue-fucked him, his hips pumping back and forth in a rocking motion.

After removing his tongue from Joseph's ass, Stephen sat on his heels then reached for the condom and lube.

"Get up on all fours."

Joseph swallowed. He was so turned on and Stephen's commands only added to his pleasure. His love, *their* love—made everything thrilling.

Once he'd positioned himself, the sensation of cool drops of liquid on his exposed hole made him startle. With a sigh, he relaxed into the familiar feel of Stephen's fingers exploring him from the inside.

His position was perfect for Stephen to stimulate his gland, and with each brush over the sensitive spot, sparks danced like electricity across his spine and into his groin. The erotic feel was almost overwhelming, and he pushed against Stephen's questing hand, aching to be filled even more.

Stephen removed his fingers and Joseph's breathing sped up. He prepared himself to feel his lover inside him, knowing it would be wonderful—that Stephen would take care with him—yet the old fears still threatened to intrude.

The large head of Stephen's cock pressed against his opening, accompanied by a soothing caress across his lower back. "Just remember how much I love you, Joseph. How dear you are to me."

The hand Stephen had used to caress his back fell to Joseph's hip. With a quick thrust, Stephen pushed his thick cock into Joseph's ass. Joseph worked to keep his breathing steady, to not clench against the intrusion.

Stephen eased himself deeper with a few more moves until he was seated all the way in Joseph's ass. Stephen stilled, using both hands to soothe and pet his ass cheeks and back, while holding himself deep inside Joseph.

Joseph was full, stretched open, but he'd been filled like this before. However, it had never been with love. Even with the slight a burn, he was still incredibly excited. He knew that once Stephen moved in him, he would feel the pressure on his prostate, and it would make their joining wonderful.

"Fuck me, Stephen," Joseph growled out. "You feel incredible."

Stephen grabbed his hips, then set up a steady rhythm of plunging into Joseph's ass, taking special care to bear down where it excited him the most. The pace increased and Joseph's sleet leaked, a tiny string of pre-cum leaking on the sheets.

All his attention was focused on what was happening inside his ass, Stephen's thrusts becoming more powerful and unrelenting. It didn't frighten him, only thrilled him. The fire

Guarded Desires

in his groin built and rose, carrying him along a cresting wave until he screamed out, his seed spilling on the bed.

His release unleashed Stephen's and he experienced a wonderful pulsing sensation inside him. Joseph couldn't believe he came without ever being touched.

Stephen pulled out, motioning with a hand on Joseph's side for him to lie down. He disposed of the condom and lay next to him, gathering him in his arms. As Stephen lazily kissed him, Joseph could sense the love he was trying to convey.

Stephen broke the connection then gazed into Joseph's eyes. He stroked the side of Joseph's face, a smile playing at the corners of his mouth.

"You came."

Joseph's face heated. "Yeah. It happened out of nowhere, I couldn't stop it."

Stephen grinned. "Objective achieved. It means I fucked you good and proper."

"Yeah?"

He chuckled. "I'm not saying it'll always be like that, but it won't be the way it was before—*that* I can promise."

Joseph snuggled closer to Stephen. "I know." He petted Stephen's furry chest. "But you can top me anytime."

Stephen chuckled again. "Feeling's mutual."

They lay together in silence for a few minutes, lazily stroking each other's arms.

"So, tell me. Has anyone ever called you Joe?"

"No. Anyone ever call you Steve?"

"Hell no."

Joseph drew his eyebrows together. "Why do you ask?"

Stephen pressed a kiss against to Joseph's head. "I don't care how small or seemingly insignificant something is, I want to know everything about you."

Joseph sighed, rubbing his face against the soft beard of the man he loved more than anything in the world. "I feel the same."

* * *

Thank you for reading Stephen and Joseph's romantic journey to a forever after! Are you ready for more sexy first responders and uniformed men from Mesa, Arizona? Then be sure to pick up, *Dangerous Wish* for Dan's story. When Joseph introduces him to a party boy who's the most beautiful man Dan's ever seen, he falls fast and hard. Unfortunately, Jared isn't into anything more than a good time. Will these two men ever find their way to each other and a happily-ever-after? Read on for a peek at the first chapter:

Crouching on the unforgiving asphalt digging into his knees, Jared Li peered under his ambulance. His gaze rested on his partner and fellow EMT, Sam, lying on his back, not moving. Jared slapped a hand over his mouth to keep from crying out. When the shots had exploded all around them, they'd both scrambled for the cover of the van. It wasn't until the cacophony had ceased that Jared had realized that Sam wasn't beside him.

His heart felt as if it were pounding in his throat, and he struggled to catch his breath. There had been times in the past where he'd felt threatened by the circumstances of an emergency call, but this was by far the worst. However, what he really needed to do was pull himself together and do what he could to help Sam.

Jared's medical training told him his fear response was paralyzing him and the adrenaline coursing through him was interfering with his ability to stay calm and think clearly. But

Guarded Desires

he also knew he needed to take advantage of it to give him the strength he'd need to get his partner out of harm's way.

He closed his eyes and forced himself to take deep, controlled breaths. His internal dialog reassured him help was likely on the way and his fellow medic was his main objective. All he had to do was focus on getting to Sam.

After opening his eyes again, he glanced around, trying to ascertain exactly where the gunfire had come from. When they'd received the call from dispatch, it hadn't stood out as being that out of the ordinary. They'd been informed that a woman was requesting assistance—that she thought her husband might have taken too many sleeping pills. The address had been practically around the corner, so they were the first to arrive.

However, as soon as they'd exited the ambulance then walked toward the home, shots had sounded, and they'd hit the ground. Jared still had no idea what could have instigated the attack.

For the past sixty seconds as he'd gathered himself, he'd hoped that Mesa Fire and Medical would appear. He knew the men and women from Engine 221 well, and they were also the closest station. Since Jared and Sam worked for a private ambulance service, there were many times when they would cross paths with their compatriots. And right now? He could really use their support. Mesa Police should've picked up the initial call as well.

God only knows what other calls they might be on. This one didn't seem that critical.

Not knowing what the extent of Sam's injuries might be meant he had to make an immediate move. He couldn't wait any longer. Taking another deep breath, Jared checked his surroundings one more time then bolted out from behind the vehicle, racing to where Sam lay.

When he reached him, another shot ricocheted off the ground nearby. Jared blocked it out. He shoved his hands under his partner's arms then dragged him by his shoulders— desperate to get them both out of the range of gunfire. As he gasped for breath from the strain of hefting Sam's dead weight, he had the sudden thought that he wished he were more of a hunky, alpha-male type of a guy. Despite his rigorous workout sessions, his slight, twinky frame could only support so much in the way of muscles.

Blood oozed from a wound in Sam's upper abdomen and Jared was frantic to get them to safety so he could work on his partner. The distant sounds of multiple sirens could be heard approaching. Breathing a sigh of relief had never before held so much meaning.

Grunting and sweating, he pulled Sam behind the cover of the ambulance. Three police cruisers screeched to a stop almost simultaneously, the piercing wail of the sirens continuing even as the officers burst from their vehicles, guns drawn. Chaos erupted with the exchange of more gunfire, but with the cops on the scene, Jared could turn his complete attention to his injured partner. Thankfully, they were well shielded at the rear of the van where Jared had access to his medical kits.

Sam remained unconscious while Jared frantically worked on him, checking his vitals then cutting away the shirt of his uniform. Without additional medical personnel to help him, all he could do was stabilize Sam as best he could and stem the bleeding. No other emergency responders would be allowed on scene until the immediate threat had passed.

Leaning his back against the bumper of the ambulance, Jared held Sam's hand. His pulse was steady, but his blood pressure was on the low side. He needed to get him transported quickly or things could go south fast. Jared stared up at the sky, a few wispy clouds blowing overhead. The late January

Guarded Desires

weather was cool, but not uncomfortable. It was preferable to the scorching heat of the Arizona summer, especially given the current circumstances.

At last, things appeared to be quietening down a little, and he chanced a peek around the truck. There was still plenty of activity, but he hadn't heard any more gunfire for a few minutes and the police sirens had finally been turned off. Jared squinted, trying to get a better view of the situation.

A heavy-set, middle-aged man was being led in handcuffs by two police officers from the house where he and Sam had originally pulled up. Jared was itching to find out what it had all been about, but Sam needed to be taken care of first.

The sound of more sirens approaching grabbed Jared's attention. He was certain that they signaled the approach of Mesa Fire and Medical. He'd never been so anxious to see his paramedic buddies as well as their more advanced equipment. If anyone could give Sam a chance, it would be them.

Jared shot to his feet to flag them over. Sure enough, it was Engine 221. Laura, the engineer, jumped down from the truck and ran over to him. She knew Sam as well as he did, but lately, Jared suspected there might be more than a fellow worker bond. Their captain, Mitchell, was close on her heels.

As soon as she reached them, Laura dropped to her knees. She threw her hands over her mouth in what seemed to be an effort to catch a sob. Mitchell halted next to her and appeared to be assessing the situation. He glanced at Jared with a grim expression, his brow furrowed, lips set in a tight line.

"Why don't you let Jared and I take over here, Laura. Now that the scene has been secured, I need you to go with Paul and Cheryl to check on the woman inside the home."

She visibly shook then took a deep breath, likely calming herself the way Jared had done. Without hesitating any further, she stood. Placing a hand on Mitchell's arm, she looked intently at him.

"I know you'll take good care of him for me."

Jared noted the unshed tears in her eyes. No doubt existed in his mind that there was more going on between them than a friendship. Mitchell nodded at her once then she took off after her fellow medics into the home where the shooting had occurred. Mitchell sighed then faced Jared.

"Is he stable enough for transport?"

"Yeah. But I thought you guys might be able to do something... Something more to make sure... You know, with your additional equipment..."

Shit. I can't lose it.

Mitchell regarded him with obvious compassion.

"I'll help you get the stretcher out then call Cheryl out here to ride with him in the back. If it'll make you feel better, I can verify that he's ready to move, but you're one of the best there is. I'm sure whatever could be done already has been handled." He clasped Jared's shoulder. "Right now, I think the sooner we get him to the hospital, the better."

Jared nodded. He was confident in his abilities—Mitchell had openly hinted more than once that they could use him over at one of the Mesa stations. However, he also knew that his personal relationship with Sam could color his judgment.

They worked together to get Sam aboard the ambulance, and by the time he was ready to jet out of there, Cheryl was already in the back of the truck monitoring Sam's condition. Gripping the wheel of the van, he hit the gas pedal and sped toward the Desert Medical Center. Toward what he hoped would be Sam's saviors.

* * *

Guarded Desires

"Come on, Dan, it'll be fun."

Dan Harrison frowned at his fellow Guardsman, Joseph Pirelli. The idea of going to a karaoke bar and making an ass of himself sounded like anything *but* fun. He knew Joseph was only trying to help—he'd been begging his friend to help him because of how socially challenged he was.

Plus, he'd only been out for a short time, so he seriously had no idea how to go about meeting guys. He'd never been that successful with girls either, as he tended to keep to himself. But he had no clue how to approach a man without it coming across as nothing more than a come-on for sex.

So far, Joseph hadn't had much luck in getting him a date. Dan appreciated his continued efforts—however, he'd hoped for a potentially less humiliating plan. Joseph's latest scheme involved an EMT he knew whose dance card was always filled and who was willing to give Dan expert dating advice.

Dan wasn't convinced that was such a great idea.

"Couldn't you and Stephen have one of your legendary barbecues instead and invite this Jared guy over? You know, something less goofy than a karaoke bar?"

Joseph punched Dan's shoulder lightly. "Hey, don't mock the singing prowess of either me or my man. And how is a barbecue any less goofy than karaoke?" Joseph frowned. "Never mind, I answered my own question. But I still think you should go. Stephen and I always have a blast when we do."

Dan tried to ignore the annoying stab of jealousy that stung him. He'd only managed to admit to himself that he was gay a mere six months before, yet he longed for what Joseph and Stephen had together. Their bond was undeniable and beautiful.

His cheeks heated as he thought of it. As a barely twenty–two-year-old guy who had only recently come to terms with his sexuality, it would make more sense for him to play around for a while, see what was out there. After all, he still had his whole life before him.

However, he wasn't that guy, and he was uncomfortable going to a gay bar alone or trolling Internet dating sites in order to hook up with someone.

"I know you said Jared would be a good person for me to get to know and all that, but do you really think he'll want me tagging along like some sort of kid brother when he goes out?"

The main reason Joseph had suggested the karaoke club was because Jared went there a lot, too. Supposedly, the EMT was willing to be Dan's dating mentor.

Dan rubbed the back of his neck. "And anyway, I hate this whole thing of trying to meet a guy, going through all that bullshit only to find out all they want is a quick blow job. I didn't even like that kind of thing when I was making myself go out with girls."

Joseph snorted. "You used to give blow jobs to girls? That's weird."

Dan covered his face with both hands in frustration. Dropping them, he glared at his friend, who was laughing and holding his stomach.

"Dude. You're starting to piss me off."

"Sorry, sorry. Oh my God, that was good. Okay, seriously, though. You need to make yourself go out. The choices when you stay at the armory for your weekend every month aren't exactly platinum. And the ones we dealt with down in Nogales? Yeah, those goons took bigotry to horrid new levels."

Dan couldn't deny the wisdom of Joseph's words. The whole 'Don't Ask, Don't Tell' policy may have fallen by the wayside, but all bigotry hadn't. The men and women who had enlisted in the Guard came from all walks of life and locations throughout the country. There were those who had no issues about being enlisted with a gay man. However, there were still

Guarded Desires

plenty of people in the armed forces who adamantly held onto their long-held prejudices.

Sighing, he internally gave in to defeat. At least he wouldn't be sitting around the small bedroom of his tiny apartment like he usually did. There were only so many PlayStation games he could play in one week, and his dishwasher job only took up about four days of said week. At least when he'd been on active duty at the Nogales, AZ border to support the Customs and Border Protection officers against a drug cartel, there'd been the opportunity to use some of his training.

In reality, the best part of that had been meeting Joseph. Finally, there had been someone he could talk to about all the competing emotions battling inside him since he'd come out. His decision to out himself had been freeing, scary and sad, all at once.

The sad part was how his parents had been so obviously disappointed. Maybe it was because he was their only child. Or maybe it was because they were very conservative. There hadn't been much in the way of a deep discussion to give him any real insight. Only an awkward hug from them both and his dad no longer being able to look him in the eye.

"Well? Am I going to have to tie you up and throw you in the trunk?"

Dan chuckled. "Fine, I surrender. But I'm *not* singing."

"Don't underestimate the power of beer. It has been known to unleash more than one wannabe rock or country star on the crowds of Jammin' Jimmy's."

"No way. Not me."

Joseph scrambled to his feet from where he'd been sitting cross-legged on Dan's living room floor.

"Let's pick out what you're going to wear."

"You're kidding, right?"

Joseph crossed his arms and narrowed his eyes.

"Don't make me drag you into the next room and force you to be fashionable, soldier."

Dan snorted. "As if you're such a fashionista. And anyway, what'll you do if I don't?"

"I'll announce to the crowd at Jimmy's that you sound exactly like Wayne Newton, and you want to perform *Danke Schoen*. Then I'll have Ted, the host, place the spotlight on you."

"You're evil."

Dan had to laugh. Joseph could get as excited as a kid on occasion, but he also had a crazy sense of humor. The banter between him and Stephen was so entertaining that he forgot to join in the conversation sometimes. On the few occasions when Rigo—Stephen's partner from the Phoenix DEA's office—would hang out with them, it was like a non-stop snarkfest.

"Yes, forcing you to wear something other than a T-shirt and jeans is all part of my evil plan."

"Ah, so you admit it. Okay, Calvin Klein, get me ready for this karaoke nightmare."

They were headed to Dan's bedroom, but Joseph turned on his heels. He stopped, glaring at Dan.

"Listen, Harrison, you are going to have fun tonight, dammit." He poked his finger in Dan's chest. "So don't give me any trouble."

Dan raised both hands. "No trouble, I swear."

Joseph nodded curtly, then marched toward the bedroom again. Dan followed behind him mumbling under his breath.

"And no singing either."

Joseph tossed over his shoulder, "I heard that!"

* * *

To keep reading, grab your copy of *Dangerous Wish* now!

Also by Morticia Knight

Sin City Uniforms

All Fired Up (Sin City Uniforms 1)

Copping an Attitude (Sin City Uniforms 2)

Justice Prevails (Sin City Uniforms 3)

Held Hostage (Sin City Uniforms 4)

Negotiating Love (Sin City Uniforms 5)

Searching for Shelter (Sin City Uniforms 6)

Strip Search (Sin City Uniforms 7)

Command & Care

Boy Issues (Command & Care 1)

Born Daddy (Command & Care 2)

His Middle (Command & Care 3)

Step Daddy (Command & Care 4)

Diva Pop (Command & Care 5)

Pretty Puppy (Command & Care 6)

Club Sensation

Master Zane's Boys

Father Series

In the Name of the Father (Father Series 1)

For the Love of a Boy (Father Series 2)

Now and Forever (Father Series 3)

Kiss of Leather

Building Bonds (Kiss of Leather 1)

Safe Limits (Kiss of Leather 2)

Bondage Rescue (Kiss of Leather 3)

Grand Opening (Kiss of Leather 4)

Gaining Trust (Kiss of Leather 5)

Cutting Cords (Kiss of Leather 6)

Facing Fears (Kiss of Leather 7)

Switching Places (Kiss of Leather 8)

Kink Aware (Kiss of Leather 9)

Soul Match

Slave for Two (Soul Match 1)

Cherished by Two (Soul Match 2)

Hiding from Two (Soul Match 3)

Surrendering for Two (Soul Match 4)

Fighting for All (Soul Match 5)

The Play Series

Role Play (Play Series 1)
Bondage Play (Play Series 2)
Pain Play (Play Series 3)

The Hampton Road Club

Hesitant Heart (The Hampton Road Club 1)
Rules of Love (The Hampton Road Club 2)
Fear of Surrender (The Hampton Road Club 3)
Mastering Love (The Hampton Road Club 4)
Begging to Serve (The Hampton Road Club 5)
Finding Sanctuary (The Hampton Road Club 6)

Hampton Road Novellas

A Master for Michael
A New Beginning for Angelo

Uniform Encounters

Secret Fire
Arresting Behavior
Love Emergency

Guarded Desire

Dangerous Wish

Single Titles

Rocked Hard

Biking Bad

Strict Consequences

VIP Access

Dear Daddy, Please Keep Me

His Boy to Hold

Brutal

Slippery When Wet

A Cutie for Kinkmas

Prancing With Daddy

About the Author

USA Today Bestselling and award-winning author Morticia Knight spends most of her nights writing about men loving men forever after. If there happens to be some friendly bondage or floggings involved, she doesn't begrudge her characters whatever their filthy little heart's desire. Even though she's been crafting her naughty tales for more years than she'd like to share —her adventures as a published author began in 2011. With over 70 gay/bisexual romance books and stories published through Knight Ever After Publishing and Pride Publishing, Morticia is bound to have something for your sexy HEA reading pleasure!

Morticia resides on the North Oregon coast where the fierce winter storms, gray skies and ocean views all conspire to spark her endless imagination.

Visit Morticia at www.morticiaknight.com

Printed in Great Britain
by Amazon